"What did you come here for?" Corinna asked bluntly.

He didn't hesitate. "To see you. To ask you about having dinner with me tonight. Just the two of us."

Her heart leaped with unexpected pleasure, yet she was careful to hide it in her words. "I had dinner with you last night."

"What does that hurt?"

She decided to be truthful with him. "Seth—after last night—I don't think it would be wise to go out with you."

His hand tightened on hers. "Don't be scared, Corinna," he said gently. "Last night was nice. Very nice. And you know it."

Yes, she did know it, and everything inside of her wanted to experience it all again, to be with this man that had lingered in her thoughts for nearly two decades.

"I can see why you became a Texas Ranger," she commented wryly. "You like to live dangerously."

Dear Reader,

We're smack in the middle of summer, which can only mean long, lazy days at the beach. And do we have some fantastic books for you to bring along! We begin this month with a new continuity, only in Special Edition, called THE PARKS EMPIRE, a tale of secrets and lies, love and revenge. And Laurie Paige opens the series with *Romancing the Enemy.* A schoolteacher who wants to avenge herself against the man who ruined her family decides to move next door to the man's son. But things don't go exactly as planned, as she finds herself falling…for the enemy.

Stella Bagwell continues her MEN OF THE WEST miniseries with *Her Texas Ranger,* in which an officer who's come home to investigate a murder finds complications in the form of the girl he loved in high school. Victoria Pade begins her NORTHBRIDGE NUPTIALS miniseries, revolving around a town famed for its weddings, with *Babies in the Bargain.* When a woman hoping to reunite with her estranged sister finds instead her widowed husband and her children, she winds up playing nanny to the whole crew. Can wife and mother be far behind? THE KENDRICKS OF CAMELOT by Christine Flynn concludes with *Prodigal Prince Charming,* in which a wealthy playboy tries to help a struggling caterer with her business and becomes much more than just her business partner in the process. Brand-new author Mary J. Forbes debuts with *A Forever Family,* featuring a single doctor dad and the woman he hires to work for him. And the MEN OF THE CHEROKEE ROSE miniseries by Janis Reams Hudson continues with *The Other Brother,* in which a woman who always counted her handsome neighbor as one of her best friends suddenly finds herself looking at him in a new light.

Happy reading! And come back next month for six new fabulous books, all from Silhouette Special Edition.

Gail Chasan
Senior Editor

Please address questions and book requests to:
Silhouette Reader Service
U.S.: 3010 Walden Ave., P.O. Box 1325, Buffalo, NY 14269
Canadian: P.O. Box 609, Fort Erie, Ont. L2A 5X3

Her Texas Ranger

STELLA BAGWELL

Silhouette®

SPECIAL EDITION®

Published by Silhouette Books

America's Publisher of Contemporary Romance

In memory of my father, Louis Copeland Cook,
a believer in doing things right. I hope he thinks I have.

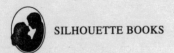

SILHOUETTE BOOKS

ISBN 0-373-24622-6

HER TEXAS RANGER

Copyright © 2004 by Stella Bagwell

Visit Silhouette Books at www.eHarlequin.com

Printed in U.S.A.

STELLA BAGWELL

sold her first book to Silhouette in November 1985. More than forty novels later, she still loves her job and says she isn't completely content unless she's writing. Recently, she and her husband of thirty years moved from the hills of Oklahoma to Seadrift, Texas, a sleepy little fishing town located on the coastal bend. Stella says the water, the tropical climate and the seabirds make it a lovely place to let her imagination soar and to put the stories in her head down on paper.

She and her husband have one son, Jason, who lives and teaches high school math in nearby Port Lavaca.

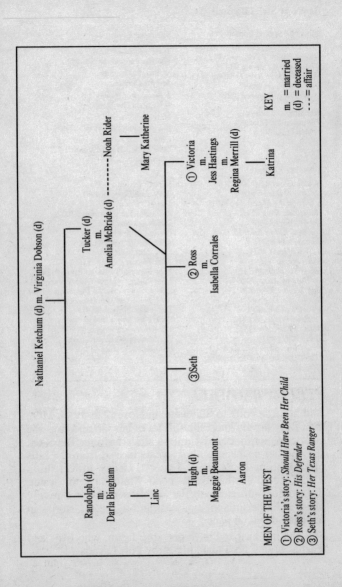

Nathaniel Ketchum (d) m. Virginia Dobson (d)

Randolph (d)
m.
Darla Bingham

Linc

Tucker (d)
m.
Amelia McBride (d) - - - - - - Noah Rider

Mary Katherine

Hugh (d)
m.
Maggie Beaumont

Aaron

③Seth

② Ross
m.
Isabella Corrales

① Victoria
m.
Jess Hastings
m.
Regina Merrill (d)

Katrina

MEN OF THE WEST

① Victoria's story: *Should Have Been Her Child*
② Ross's story: *His Defender*
③ Seth's story: *Her Texas Ranger*

KEY

m. = married
(d) = deceased
- - - = affair

Chapter One

"One riot, one Ranger. Isn't that the reputation you Rangers have down in Texas?"

The question prompted Seth Ketchum to cast a wry glance at his younger brother, Ross, who was standing just to the right of his chair.

Seth had almost forgotten what it was like to be back on the T Bar K with his family. Two years had passed since he'd seen his brother and sister. The time had slipped up on him and now as they crowded around him in the living room of the ranch house, he realized just how much he'd missed his siblings.

"That's what the saying is—one riot, one Ranger," Seth responded to his brother's comment. "But I'm not a superhero, Ross."

Ross reached down and slapped his brother proudly on the back. "That's right, Seth. You're better than a superhero. You don't have to waste time racing into a telephone booth to change out of your boots and hat.''

A few feet away, from her seat on a leather chester-field couch, their sister, Victoria, groaned. ''Ross, this mess isn't funny. I don't know how you can joke at a time like this.''

Ross chuckled as he continued to squeeze Seth's shoulder. ''Who's joking?'' Ross retorted. ''Company D down in San Antonio would fall apart without Seth.''

The two men were dressed similarly in boots and jeans and long-sleeved cotton shirts. As far as resembling each other, Seth was a fraction shorter and more solidly built than his six-foot brother. Where Ross's hair was nearly black, Seth's was a dozen shades of brown, ranging from light to dark. But the most striking difference in the men was in their demeanor. Ross was normally all grins and teasing laughter whereas Seth had always been a quiet, serious man.

''Ross, your confidence in me is a little exaggerated,'' Seth countered. ''At least my captain would say so.''

Grinning, Ross waved away his older brother's modest remark.

''You're already a sergeant. Before long you'll be a captain.''

Seth grimaced. Ross was still, in many ways, just like their late father, Tucker. He'd believed all Ketchums were meant to go straight to the top of the ladder.

''I don't want to be a captain,'' Seth said while gazing absently at the glass of iced tea he was holding. ''I like the position I'm in just fine.''

''Seth, you—''

''Ross, will you let it rest?'' Victoria interrupted. ''Seth isn't telling you how to run the ranch. And he's only been home a few minutes! Why don't you let him catch his breath?''

Seth glanced gratefully at Victoria. She was not only a beautiful woman, she was also a damn good doctor and as far as he was concerned, she'd always been the most levelheaded of the four Ketchum siblings. After all these years of her being single, he found it hard to believe that she and Jess Hastings had mended their differences and were now married and expecting a child. Yet that wasn't nearly the shock he'd received when he'd heard that his playboy brother had tied the knot with Isabella Corrales, a beautiful lawyer from the Jicarilla Apache reservation.

But romance and weddings hadn't been the only things taking place on the T Bar K. Jess, his new brother-in-law and undersheriff of San Juan County, had been shot and nearly killed. Thankfully, that case had been solved and the ranch hand that had committed the crime was now serving time behind bars. However, there was still the mystery of the murdered foreman, Noah Rider, to unravel and everyone in the family was now looking to Seth, expecting him to work a miracle in a case that, frankly, had been cold from the very beginning.

Ross moved away from Seth and took a seat on the arm of his wife's chair. ''I just want to brag a little on my brother, sis,'' he said to Victoria. ''I'm not trying to tell him how to do his job. Hell, that's the reason we called him. He knows how to investigate a murder case. We don't. That is, except for Jess. But he's already said the San Juan County Sheriff's Department is welcoming all the help they can get.''

Seth said, ''Well, like I told you both on the phone,

New Mexico isn't exactly my jurisdiction, unless we have a Texas crime that overflows into this state.''

"It appears that you have," Victoria spoke up. "Noah Rider lived in Hereford, Texas, at the time he was murdered. Looks to me like a Texas Ranger has every right to investigate the death of a citizen of Texas.''

A faint grin lifted the corner of Seth's lips. "Depending on where that death occurred," he told his sister.

"We don't know where the death occurred," Isabella pointed out.

Ross smiled proudly at his wife. "Good point, honey. I think I'll keep you around, after all."

Bemused, Seth watched his brother lift the back of Isabella's hand to his lips. He'd never seen Ross acting so smitten and it came as a shock that his brother was really and truly in love with someone other than himself.

"Seth, you don't really have to have jurisdiction around here to do a little snooping on your own, do you?" Victoria asked, her face wrinkled with concern. "I mean, you don't have to work in conjunction with Jess's office, do you?"

Seth smiled briefly at his sister. One of the reasons he'd dropped everything back in Texas and hurried out here to the T Bar K was to help ease Victoria's mind. From what Ross had told him, Victoria had been extremely upset from the very onset of this whole murder thing and she'd continued to worry about what it might do to the family, and the ranch, if the killer wasn't caught and brought to justice. All the anxiety couldn't be good for the baby she was carrying. And more than anything, Seth wanted to see his sister deliver a healthy child.

"Don't worry, Victoria. I can snoop in a way that won't step on anyone's toes. I just won't have immediate access to Ranger computer data. But if I need something searched, I have a friend back in Texas who'll do it for me."

"A female friend?" Ross asked impishly.

Seth didn't bother to glance at his brother. After all these years, he was used to Ross's teasing. And now that Seth was thirty-nine, nearing forty, and still single, he expected to hear more from his newly married brother.

"No. A fellow Ranger."

"Seth, you're just no fun at all."

"I didn't come up here for fun, little brother."

Instead of taking offense, Ross chuckled. "Okay, you don't have any fun back in Texas and you don't plan on having any while you're here at home. So what are you planning to do?"

The question brought Seth's head around and he looked at his brother squarely. "I plan to track down Noah's killer."

The next morning Seth was up early. After eating a big breakfast with his brother, he walked out to the front porch and there he stayed, long after Ross headed on down to the barn to start his day's work.

He'd nearly forgotten how dry it was up here in northern New Mexico. It was such a switch from humid San Antonio that his eyes burned and the inside of his nose felt as if it was going to crack.

But it was beautiful here on the ranch. He could never deny that, he thought as he watched the sun burst over the crest of eastern mountains. It was wild and rugged land that was as harsh as the climate could be. He'd left the ranch nearly eighteen years ago when he'd been only twenty-one.

At the time, Tucker had thrown a walleyed fit. Which had been no surprise to anyone in the family, especially not Seth. His father had been a hard man with his own ideas about how to live life and how he wanted his sons and daughter to live it. The last thing Tucker had wanted was for Seth to pursue a career in law enforcement. Particularly, a Texas Ranger, which would force him to leave the state. But Seth had defied his father and followed his dream. He'd become a member of an elite group of lawmen, a feat that very few men accomplish in a whole lifetime. And he'd done it all on his own, without the help of Tucker Ketchum. A fact that left him full of pride, but always a little sad, too.

"So here you are."

At the sound of Marina's voice, Seth turned to see the heavyset cook step from the doorway and onto the wooden planked porch. The Mexican woman had worked for the Ketchum family for forty or more years and was considered more of a family member than an employee. Ross kept her wrapped around his little finger, but she always seemed overjoyed to see Seth, whenever he did make a rare trip up here to the ranch.

"Did you need me for something, Marina?"

She grinned at him as though just looking at him made her happy and he felt a pang of guilt for not keeping in closer touch with his family.

"I just make a fresh pot of coffee," she said. "You like some?"

Nearly an hour had passed since Seth had eaten breakfast. He supposed he could use a little more caffeine and it would give him an opportunity to throw a few questions at Marina.

He followed the old cook through the large, rambling house, to the back where the kitchen was located. The room was warm, the breakfast mess already cleaned away from the long pine table, but the smell of fried bacon still lingered in the air, mixing with the scent of freshly brewed coffee. From atop the refrigerator, a small radio was playing country music and reporting tidbits of local news.

Aside from a few updated appliances, the room was the same as it had been when he'd been a child. Except that his mother wasn't hovering behind his chair, ruffling his hair and reminding him to eat his oats.

His parents had been dead for some years now, along with his brother, Hugh. His brother had been the first to go—six years ago, he'd been gored to death by one of the ranch's bulls. A year later, his mother had passed away from the lingering complications of a stroke, then a little more than a year ago, his father had died from heart failure. A big part of his family was gone now.

Shoving away the bittersweet memories, he caught Marina's attention and patted the seat kitty-corner to his left. "Pour yourself a cup, too, Marina, and come sit here beside me."

Marina eyed him with curious black eyes as she lifted the tail of her white apron and wiped her hands.

"I don't need to sit. I got work to do."

"You're going to sit. This place won't fall apart if you rest for a few minutes."

Mumbling under her breath, she poured the coffee, then carried the two mugs over to the table.

"What's the matter?" he asked as she eased down in the chair. "Don't you want to visit with me?"

She pushed one of the coffee mugs toward him. "You don't want to visit. You want to ask me questions. About the murder."

A low chuckle rumbled up from his chest. "How do you know that? I haven't said anything yet."

She frowned. "I see the look on your face. I know you, Seth Ketchum. You might as well pin that badge of yours on your chest."

He touched his hand to the left of his chest just above his shirt pocket. It wasn't very often that he went without his Ranger badge. But he was basically on vacation now and as he'd told Victoria, he didn't want to step on any toes up here in New Mexico.

"I'm not going to ask you about the murder, Marina. You couldn't know anything about it anyway."

Her frown deepened as though she wasn't sure if he'd just insulted her. "Well then—what we gonna talk about? You?"

Seth chuckled again. "No. You already know all there is to know about me." He lifted the mug to his lips, took a careful sip and lowered it back to the tabletop. "How's your memory, Marina?"

She grinned and relaxed against the back of the wooden chair. "I remember you got a little brown birthmark on your hip."

"You don't have to go that far back," he said dryly. "Just back to the time when Noah Rider was foreman here on the T Bar K."

"I can do that. What you want to know about him?"

Seth shook his head. "Not him. I want you to try to remember anyone and everyone that Dad had feuds with back at that time."

"Oh, Lord," she groaned. "Looks like we're gonna be here a while."

* * *

Later that afternoon, Seth stared at the list he and Marina had compiled. He wasn't sure why he felt that his father was somehow connected to the murder. It wasn't that he thought Tucker capable of killing anyone, even in the heat of one of his rages. And anyway, Tucker was dead, he couldn't have killed Noah. But Tucker and Noah had been close. The foreman had always backed Tucker in anything and everything. The two of them together might have angered someone so badly they'd sworn revenge. It didn't make a whole lot of sense. Especially since no one had attempted to kill Tucker. But then as far as Seth was concerned, homicide never made any sense.

Fifteen names were on the list. Yet there was only one that generated much of his interest. Rube Dawson. From what Ross had told him at lunch, Rube was still a neighbor. And as far as Ross was concerned, the old man was the last person to be involved in Noah's death. But it was far too early for Seth to exclude anyone from the list. Especially when he remembered very well that Tucker and Rube had once had a big squabble over the ownership of a racehorse.

Stuffing the list in his pocket, he went out to the kitchen and told Marina he'd be gone for a while. Outside, he climbed in his black pickup truck and headed off the T Bar K. When he reached the point where the ranch road branched with the main county road, he turned to the right in the direction of Rube Dawson's place.

Twenty minutes later, he pulled onto a red dirt road, rumbled across a cattle guard, then drove a quarter mile through foothills dotted with green juniper and piñon pine.

When the Dawson homestead finally came into view, Seth was taken aback. Even though it had been many years since he'd visited the place with his father, he'd not imagined it would look like this. True, the Dawsons had always been on the poor side, but the present state of the place went beyond the lack of money. The small, stucco house was badly in need of paint and shingles. The barns and outbuildings were also in sad neglect with sagging roofs, missing boards and flaking paint. Fences were leaning and in some spots completely resting on the ground.

Apparently Rube wasn't lifting a finger around here, Seth thought with disgust as he parked his truck next to a dark, older-model sedan and an even older Dodge pickup truck with rusted fenders.

The moment he stepped to the ground, he was met by a white dog that appeared to be part border collie. The wag of his tail assured Seth the dog was friendly and he paused on the path to the house long enough to bend and greet the animal.

"Don't worry, mister, Cotton won't bite."

Seth glanced up to see a young boy somewhere between ten and twelve years old standing on the small front porch. Blue jeans and a baggy T-shirt covered his painfully thin body. Thick blond hair tickled his eyebrows and he swiped at it with an impatient hand as he carefully watched Seth's every move.

Leaving the dog, Seth walked over to the porch, noticing all the while that there was no yard to speak of around the house, just a few clumps of sage and hard-packed red earth.

"Hello," he said to the boy. "Does Rube Dawson still live here?"

The boy nodded as his blue eyes narrowed with wary

speculation. "Sure does. He's my grandpa. I call him Pa."

The news jolted Seth. Rube only had one child and that was Corrina. This was Corrina's child! But that shouldn't surprise him, he quickly rationalized. Years had passed since he'd left San Juan County. More than enough time for her to marry and have a son of this age.

"Do you think I might talk to him?" Seth asked.

The boy swiped once again at the corn-colored hair pestering his eyes. He needed a haircut, Seth decided, and a few good meals to put some meat on his bones.

"What'cha wanta talk to him about?"

"Matt! That isn't any way to greet a visitor!"

Seth recognized the female voice even before she stepped from behind the screen door and onto the porch. It was Corrina. And for a moment he couldn't speak or think of one sensible thing to say. After all these years he'd never expected to see her again and now that she was standing before him, he was suddenly flooded with memories of more innocent, simpler times.

"Hello, Seth," she said in a low, warm voice.

Vivid blue eyes stared back at him and he got the impression that she was just as surprised to see him as he'd been to find her here on this broken-down ranch.

Stepping up on the porch, he offered her his hand. "Hello, Corrina. How are you?"

He could sense her hesitation, then finally she reached up and slipped her hand into his. The contact was brief, but long enough to feel her work-roughed palm.

Her eyes darted down and away from him as her fingers reached up to the tangle of chestnut curls brushing her shoulders. "I'm…fine, Seth. Just fine."

She looked back at him and Seth watched with bemusement as faint pink color swept across her cheeks. If finding him on the doorstep was embarrassing to her, he couldn't imagine why. He'd not seen her in twenty years and even then the two of them had been little more than acquaintances who'd sometimes talked with each other at school. There was no way she could have ever known that he'd had a crush on her. Because he'd not told anyone about it. Especially not her.

Seth smiled, hoping to ease the tension he could see in her slender body. "That's good. I'm…surprised to see you here."

She let out a nervous little laugh, glanced at the boy, then back to Seth again. "Probably not as surprised as I am to see you." She rubbed her palms down the front of her jeans. "Uh—what are you doing here?"

He cleared his throat as he felt Corrina's son watching him closely. "I wanted to talk to Rube. I thought he might be able to give me some…help."

"Help?" Corrina repeated blankly.

She was just as pretty as he remembered, Seth thought. Maybe even prettier now that the years had matured her into a woman. Her skin was milky white, making her blue eyes even more vibrant. The riot of curls teasing her shoulders was thick and unruly, their color consisting of myriad shades varying from cinnamon to ginger. A few errant strands clung to her high cheekbone and he watched her brush them away with the same impatient gesture as her son's.

"Yeah," he answered. "I guess you've heard about all the trouble over at the T Bar K?"

She nodded and he found himself looking at her lips—full and soft, their mauve color dark against her white teeth. Did she have a husband? he wondered.

There was no ring on her hand. But that didn't mean some man hadn't put his brand on her in another way. Matt was proof of that.

"Yes," she answered. "It's pretty much been the talk of the county. I'm sorry, Seth. I'm sure the whole thing has been hard on your family."

Matt came to stand beside his mother. "How can Pa help you?"

Corrina put her arm around her son's slender shoulders. "Seth, this is my son, Matthew. We don't have much company out here, so you'll have to forgive his manners."

We don't have much company. Did she and Matthew live here? he wondered.

Seth momentarily pushed the question out of his mind and offered his hand to the sullen child. "Hello, Matthew. I'm Seth Ketchum."

Matthew was clearly pleased to be greeted as an adult rather than a child, but there was still a suspicious look in his eyes as he shook hands with Seth.

"Are you one of those rich Ketchums that live next to us?"

"Next to us" meant at least ten miles away as the crow flied, but Rube Dawson's property did butt up to a portion of the T Bar K. And out here in New Mexico it was the same as West Texas—land was usually measured in sections.

"Matt!" Corrina scolded. "It's not polite to ask someone about their finances!"

Seth merely chuckled. "Well, I'm not all that rich and part of my family lives next to you," he told Matthew. "But I don't. I live down in Texas. In San Antonio, where the Alamo is."

"Oh," Matthew mumbled, then a flicker of interest passed over his face. "Do you know Aaron?"

Seth nodded. "He's my nephew. Are you two friends?"

Matthew nodded. "Yeah. We ride the same school bus together. He's younger than me, but he's pretty cool."

"Mr. Ketchum is a Texas Ranger," Corrina said to her son.

Matt's blue eyes suddenly widened with disbelief. "You mean, like the one on TV?"

"That's right," Corrina replied. "Except that Seth is the real thing."

Matthew's mouth fell open as he stared openly at Seth. "You're not wearing a badge or gun."

Seth grinned. He didn't know why, but something about the boy touched him. Maybe it was the vulnerable look in his eyes or the way he sidled close to his mom as though he couldn't trust the outside world.

"That's because I'm here as a neighbor," Seth explained.

Corrina gestured toward the screen door leading into the house. "Dad's inside, if you'd like to talk to him," she invited.

"If he's busy I can come back some other time," Seth offered.

She cast him an odd look. "Dad's never busy. He—uh—he's retired now."

Without waiting for him to reply, she opened the door and stood to one side to allow him entry. Seth slipped past her and into a dimly lit living room packed with mismatched pieces of older furniture. The house wasn't air-conditioned, but there was a water-cooled fan blowing through vents in the ceiling. The moist breeze was enough to make the room temperature tolerable.

"Dad's sitting out on the back porch," Corrina stated as she ushered him down a short hallway and into a small kitchen with worn linoleum and white metal cabinets.

Along the back wall of the room, Corrina pushed open another screen door and motioned for Seth to follow her.

"Wake up, Dad," she said in a raised voice. "Someone is here to see you."

Rube Dawson was sitting in a metal lawn chair at one end of the screened-in cubicle. His face was red, his eyes bloodshot. Graying brown hair lay in limp hanks against his head and edged down over his ears. A blue plaid shirt was stretched taut over his rounded belly.

Seth didn't need to see the empty beer bottles sitting on the floor next to his chair to tell him that Rube was a continual drinker.

"Hello, Mr. Dawson. Remember me?"

The older man twisted his head around and squinted long and hard at Seth. "Yeah, I think I do. You're a Ketchum. Seth, isn't it?"

Seth nodded while deciding Rube apparently hadn't ruined all his brain cells with alcohol. "That's right. I'm Seth. Ross's older brother."

Nodding, Rube reached a hand toward Seth and the two men shook hands.

"Sit down, son," Rube invited warmly, "and tell me what this visit is about."

Seth took a seat in a webbed lawn chair to Rube's right. From the corner of his eye he could see Corrina lingering in the doorway, almost as if she was afraid to leave her father alone with him.

"Would you like a cup of coffee, Seth? Or some iced tea?" she offered.

He looked at her. "Tea would be nice. Thanks."

She disappeared from the doorway and Seth turned his attention to Tucker's old friend.

With slow, easy movements, he settled back in the chair and crossed his boots at the ankles. "I thought you might be able to help me, Rube. I'm up here trying to help my family find out who killed Noah Rider."

Rube grimaced and swiped a thick hand through his hair. "That was a hell of a thing. I couldn't believe it when I heard about it. Noah hadn't been around here for years. Who would have wanted to kill him?"

Seth studied him closely. "I don't suppose you'd kept in contact with him?"

Rube shook his head. "Nah. It's been about twenty-two, twenty-three years since he left here. After he left here I think I ran into him a couple of times after that. And that was by accident over at Le Mesa Park."

"What was he doing back then?"

"Training racehorses for some rancher down in Texas. Don't know where. That's been too many years ago for me to remember."

Since the remains of Noah had been discovered on the T Bar K, the San Juan County Sheriff's Department had sent Chief Deputy Daniel Redwing to Hereford, Texas, to search Noah's last known residence. Redwing hadn't found much for them to go on. The man had apparently been living a simple, modest life. From what the deputy had gathered from the man's neighbors, Noah had lived alone and rarely had visitors. At the time of his death, he'd been employed at a local feedlot. Physically demanding work for a man in his sixties.

Which could only mean that Noah hadn't possessed a nest egg for his older years. He'd been forced to work to supplement his monthly social security check, Seth mentally concluded.

"Well, at the time he was killed he was working full-time at a feedlot. His employer told a San Juan County deputy he never missed work and was surprised when Noah had told him he wanted a day off to drive up here to New Mexico."

"Hmm. So, old Noah was working," Rube said thoughtfully. "That doesn't surprise me. He was always a damn sight more ambitious than me."

That was quite an understatement, Seth decided as he focused his gaze on the back view of the Dawson place. Like the front, there was no yard, just red packed earth dotted with rocks and a few clumps of scraggy sage. Beyond, some twenty yards away, a network of broken-down corrals joined one end of the barn. Except for one black horse, the pens were empty. From the looks of things, Seth figured they'd been empty for several years.

"So you're retired now," Seth commented.

Rube leaned forward and rubbed a hand over both knees. "Yeah. I had to give up ranchin'. Just got too old and stiff to sit a saddle. And I couldn't afford to hire help. Sold off all my cattle and the horses, too."

Footsteps sounded just behind Seth and he glanced over his shoulder to see Corrina walking onto the porch carrying a tray with two glasses of iced tea.

As she approached him, her gaze met his briefly then fell swiftly to the tray in her hands.

"I hope you like it sweet," she said quietly. "I already had it made."

She bent toward him, and as he picked up one of the glasses, he caught the faint scent of flowers on her hair. The sweet fragrance reminded Seth how very long it had been since he'd took any sort of notice of a woman. "I'm sure it will be fine. Thank you, Corrina."

"I'll bet I don't have to tell you that Corrina is the light of my life," Rube said to Seth as his daughter handed him the other glass. "I don't know what I'd have done if she hadn't come to live with me. She takes care of me just like that sister of yours took care of Tucker before he died."

Seth's gaze settled on Corrina's face. Her smooth features were unmoving, giving him little or no hint to what she was thinking about her father's comments.

"I'm sure you must really appreciate your daughter," Seth replied.

Rube tilted the tea glass to his lips. After several swallows, he said, "Like I said, Corrina is the light of my life. I couldn't make it without her."

Totally ignoring her father's possessive praise, Corrina quietly walked off the porch. Inside the small kitchen, she walked to the double sink and, balancing her hands on the ledge of the counter, she bent her head and closed her eyes.

Seth Ketchum! Dear Lord, what was a sergeant in the Texas Rangers doing here?

"Mom, is something wrong?"

Matthew's voice jolted her. With a guilty start, she quickly turned to him, while carefully hiding her shaking hands behind her back. She couldn't let her son, or anyone, for that matter, know what seeing Seth Ketchum had done to her.

"No, Matt. Nothing is wrong," she lied. "Nothing at all."

Chapter Two

A few minutes later, Seth swallowed the remainder of his drink and rose to his feet. He wasn't really getting any useful information from Rube. And to be honest, the old man was not someone he cared to sit and reminisce with. He was slovenly and represented a side of life that Seth had seen all too often when dealing with criminals. Not that he thought Rube was a criminal. The only thing he figured the old man was guilty of was laziness.

"Well, thanks for your time, Rube. I'd better be going."

"Sure thing, Seth. Anytime," the old rancher replied, then squinted his eyes as another thought struck him. "Say, did Ross ever find that stallion of his?"

Seth paused at the door to look back at the old man. "You know about Snip going missing?"

"Ross called me when it first happened. He thought

I might have seen the horse. But I don't get out that much—just drive into town now and then. I told him I hadn't seen the horse."

"Well, Ross still hasn't found him," Seth said.

Rube shook his head. "That's too bad," he said regretfully. "He's probably dead by now."

Seth wondered why the old man would be thinking in that direction, when there were all sorts of scenarios that could have happened with Snip. However, he didn't question Rube. For one thing, he didn't want to appear as though he'd come over here to interrogate anyone.

"Ross isn't giving up on finding him yet," Seth told him, and then with a final word of farewell, he left Rube and entered the kitchen.

Immediately, he spotted Corrina working at the counter. He carried his empty glass to where she was standing, drying a large metal roasting pan.

"Thanks for the tea," he said. "Where would you like me to put this?"

She cut him a brief, sidelong glance. And he got the sense that his presence was making her nervous. Why, he didn't know, but the fact did intrigue him.

"Just drop it into the dishwater there in the sink."

He did as she suggested, then casually leaned a hip against the counter. "I—uh—I was very surprised to see you here, Corrina. I thought you'd left San Juan County years ago."

Corrina placed the dried pot to one side of the countertop before she turned to face him. "I was gone for a while. But when Dad started…going downhill I came back to take care of him."

Her blue eyes were shadowed with fatigue—or was it sadness? Either way, it bothered the heck out of Seth to see this beautiful woman unsmiling, her eyes dead.

"I'm sorry Rube's health is poor," he said.

Her eyes darted away from his and her hands twisted the dishcloth into a tight rope. "Well, at least he's alive. That's more than you have." She turned her gaze back on him and this time there was compassion in the blue depths. "It's still hard for me to believe that your father is gone. I'm very sorry about that, Seth. He was…quite a character around here. I think everyone misses him."

A wry smile touched Seth's lips. "I don't know that I'd go so far to say that *everyone* misses Tucker. He could be a real…difficult man at times. But you are right…. I miss my father and so do my siblings."

She nodded, then realizing she had a death hold on the dishcloth, she tossed it onto the cabinet and wiped her hands down the front of her jeans. All the while, she was thinking how strong and masculine this man looked.

Long years had passed since she and Seth had attended the same high school. Back then he'd been a handsome boy with a quiet maturity that had impressed her. Now he was a striking man with lines of character etching his chiseled lips and hazel eyes.

Even though he was dressed in jeans, boots and hat as most of the ranchers in this area, Seth's appearance would stand out from theirs, she realized. Not just because he had a long, muscled body that oozed sexuality. There was an air of authority about him that was only multiplied by the knowledge that he was a Texas Ranger.

"I…uh…never expected to see you again, Seth. You've been gone a long time."

He was surprised she'd even noticed. Or had she simply meant the term "long time" in a general way? he wondered. "Eighteen years," he answered. "But I've come home off and on throughout that time. You would have thought we'd have run into each other.''

A wan smile touched her lips in a way that said his being in San Juan County was hardly enough proximity for them to meet. ''Well…we don't exactly move in the same circles.''

He'd never been a social creature, but perhaps she believed he was. People around here had always been quick to put labels on the Ketchum family. Most of them wrong. And he supposed that hadn't changed since he'd moved away.

''I didn't know you lived here,'' he admitted. ''I'd heard that you married and moved away.''

Turning back to the counter, Corrina picked up the lid to the pot she'd just finished drying. As she swiped a dish towel over it, she said, ''Matthew's father and I are divorced. We were living in Colorado at the time and it was easier just to stay there than to make a major move. But then a couple of years ago, Dad began begging me to come back home and I…couldn't refuse him.'' She shot him a quick glance. ''What about you, Seth? Do you have a family down in Texas?''

His eyes widened, as though just someone's asking him such a question was a shock. ''Me, a family? No. I'm not a husband or a father. Just a Texas Ranger.''

She wasn't surprised. Although, looking at him, it made her wonder how he'd managed to avoid the women, who no doubt gave him second and third looks. Yet she sensed that he was a man who lived his job and anything else was put on the back burner.

Realizing she'd been holding her breath, she let it out and reached up to push back the swath of hair that had dipped onto her cheekbone. ''Well, having a family isn't always what you might expect it to be. The main thing is that you're happy.''

There was a sadness in her voice that struck Seth right in the middle of his chest. Corrina Dawson had been a soft, sweet young girl. He didn't like to think she'd already been scarred by a man. Especially one who hadn't appreciated her.

''I don't have any complaints,'' he said. Then, deciding he'd dallied in the kitchen long enough, he added, ''Well, I'd better be going, Corrina. It was nice seeing you again.''

She lifted her head and gave him a little smile. ''Yes, it was nice to see you, too. Take care, Seth.''

He nodded, then quickly found his way back to the living room, where he let himself out onto the front porch.

''Hey, Mr. Ketchum, want to see my horse?''

Seth looked around to see Corrina's young son sitting on top of a wooden doghouse just to the right of the front porch. The boy was staring at him expectantly, almost hopefully, and Seth realized there was no way he could turn down the invitation.

''Sure,'' Seth told him. ''Just show the way.''

Matthew leaped off the doghouse and motioned for Seth to follow him around the house to a beaten path that led to a nearby barn. The white dog trotted at their heels.

At the rickety corral, Matthew climbed upon the top rail of the fence, then jammed two fingers into his mouth and let out a piercing whistle.

Immediately, the black horse Seth had spotted earlier came trotting out of the building and straight up to Matthew.

''This is Blackjack. He's nice, huh?''

The gelding was a quality animal, Seth realized as he eyed the heavily built quarter horse. No doubt someone had paid a fistful of money for him.

"Very nice," Seth agreed. "You must be proud of him."

For the first time since Seth had arrived at the Dawson place, Matthew shot him a smile. "Sure am! I ride him all the time!" he exclaimed. Then just as quickly the smile faded and he ducked his head and mumbled, "That's about all there is to do around this old place."

Folding his arms against his chest, Seth rested a shoulder against the corral fence. "You don't like living here with your grandfather?"

With his head still bent, Matthew shrugged one shoulder. "Pa's all right. But he don't do nothin'. Except sit around and drink beer. That's not somethin' I want to do."

Thank God for that, Seth thought with relief. But when would that change? he wondered. How long would it be before Rube's bad habits began to influence the boy?

"It's not something you should do, either," Seth told him.

"Well, Pa says it helps the pain in his joints. Guess that makes it all right," he muttered.

Seth was trying to decide how to respond to that when Matthew was distracted by a nudge from Blackjack's nose.

The boy affectionately scratched the horse between the ears, then stroked the blaze down his face.

"Have you had Blackjack long?" Seth asked.

"Pa gave him to me last year for my tenth birthday. But I'm eleven now," he tacked on with importance. "We used to have another horse, too. A gray mare. But

Pa sold her. Said she was more trouble than she was worth.''

So Rube had bought the black gelding for his grandson, Seth mused. A generous gift from a man who apparently lived on little more than a social security check. But then Rube had sold off all his cattle, he quickly reminded himself. Perhaps he'd put a bundle in the bank and was now drawing a respectable amount of interest. However, if that was the case, he certainly wasn't using any of the money around the homestead.

"That's quite a gift," Seth commented. "Do you ever have friends over to ride with you?"

Matthew's head swung back and forth. "I can't have friends over. Mom says it would get on Pa's nerves."

A nice way of saying the boy couldn't have friends over who would see his alcoholic grandfather. What in the world was Corrina thinking? Why was she living here, subjecting her son to this type of environment?

"Well, how would you like to come over to the T Bar K and ride with me sometime soon?"

Matthew's blue eyes suddenly grew wide with wonder. "You mean it?"

Seth didn't know a whole lot about children, except that he loved them and tried to help with as many children's programs as his busy schedule would allow. It made him feel good to think he'd lifted this boy's spirits.

"Sure, I mean it. I'll call your mother in a day or two and talk to her about it. Is that okay with you?"

"Okay!"

From her window in the kitchen, Corrina watched the interplay between Seth and her son.

Matthew must have intercepted Seth before he reached his truck and talked him into going down to the barn to see Blackjack. The idea surprised her. Matt normally didn't take to strangers. Especially adults. But he'd seemed duly impressed with the fact that Seth was a Texas Ranger.

She sighed as a bittersweet feeling wound its way around her heart. When Matthew had been born, she'd wanted so much for him. Mainly two loving parents, a nice home and financial security. Yet try as she might, none of those things had come to pass.

Her son was hungry for companionship. Not just from her, but male companionship. The sort he should have been getting from his father. But Dale had walked out of their lives when Matthew had been only two years old. Her son didn't remember his father. Nor did he understand why his father hadn't wanted to be a family with them then or now.

Corrina had given up trying to understand years ago. Dale had been a dreamer and he hadn't wanted any responsibilities holding him down for any reason. He'd moved on to another life and never bothered to contact the family he'd left behind. In a way, Corrina was glad she never had to see him or deal with him over parental rights to Matthew. Yet she wasn't blind. She knew how much Matthew ached for a father and that filled her with a guilt she dealt with every day. And her father wasn't the best role model.

"Corrina, are you in there, honey?"

The sound of her father's loud call pulled her wistful gaze away from the window.

"Yes, Dad. I'm here."

"Would you bring me another pack of cigarettes? My old bones just don't want to move today."

Since Corrina's suggestions fell on deaf ears, she'd long ago stopped encouraging her father to change his habits to better his health. Yet it hurt her to see the things he was doing to himself. When Corrina had been in elementary school, her mother, June, had died suddenly and unexpectedly from a hidden heart problem. The tragedy had narrowed her already small family down to just her and Rube.

When she'd married Dale, she'd done so with the hope that his family would become hers, too. But his parents had been cold, distant people who preferred to keep to themselves. Which was just as well, she supposed. They'd never cared for her and Matthew any more than their son had.

The lack of family was the main reason Corrina had decided to come back to San Juan County and live with her father. She realized people thought she was crazy for putting up with a cantankerous old man. But he was her father. And he loved and needed her. That was more than she could say about some people's family relationships.

She opened a cabinet and pulled down a pack of her father's cigarettes. "I'll be right there, Dad."

Later that evening, as Seth and Ross walked from the cattle barn to the house, Seth used the time to toss a few questions at his younger brother. "Ross, why in hell didn't you tell me that Rube Dawson had turned into a drunkard?"

"Didn't know he had. The few times I've run into him in town, he seemed perfectly sober."

Seth snorted. "All I can say is you must not have been looking at the man."

"Well, I didn't give him a Breathalyzer test or make him walk a straight line, if that's what you mean."

Ignoring his brother's sarcasm, Seth said, "And you

could have warned me that Corrina was living out there now.''

Ross stopped in his tracks to stare at Seth. ''Didn't know that either. But why does that matter—'' He broke off, his eyebrows arched with wry speculation. ''Well, well, this is something new. My brother, the Ranger, actually noticing a woman.''

Seth shot him a withering look. ''How could I *not* notice with her living there?''

Ross could see from the tight set of Seth's jaw that his brother wasn't in any mood for joking, so he quickly sobered his own amused expression. ''I honestly didn't know Corrina lived there,'' he said, then added with a thoughtful frown, ''If I remember right, she was around my age, wasn't she?''

Seth nodded. ''I was a senior when you two were freshmen.''

''I always got the impression that she had a chip on her shoulder,'' Ross commented.

''She had reason,'' Seth countered gruffly. ''The Dawsons were always one of the poorest families around here. I'm sure it was a struggle for her to hold her head up with pride.''

''I wonder what she's doing there now. With Rube, I mean. Isn't she married?'' Ross asked.

Seth turned and continued walking in the direction of the house. Ross automatically moved into step beside him.

''Divorced. She has an eleven-year-old son, Matthew.''

Ross took his time digesting this news before he asked, ''Well, did Rube give you any helpful information about Noah?''

"Unfortunately no. Said he hadn't seen the man in several years."

"Do you believe him?"

Seth sighed. "I have no reason not to believe him. Yet." He looked at his brother. "He seems to think your stallion is dead."

Ross snorted. "Hell, that old codger doesn't know anything about Snip! Dad always said Rube knew a whole lot of nothing about a whole lot of subjects. You wasted your time going over there, brother."

Where the murder case was concerned, he probably had wasted time, Seth thought. But he'd seen Corrina again. A young woman he'd never quite been able to forget. He couldn't count that as wasted time.

The next morning, Jess called bright and early to warn Seth to get a horse saddled. The undersheriff was coming out to the ranch so that the two men could ride to the scene where the T Bar K hands had originally discovered Noah Rider's remains.

Since Jess was on duty and would be coming to the ranch in the capacity of undersheriff rather than as his brother-in-law, Seth couldn't help but be a little concerned about throwing their investigative efforts together. He didn't want Sheriff Perez to think he was trying to horn in on his business. And when Jess pulled up thirty minutes later to unload his own personal mount from a two-horse trailer, Seth was quick to convey his worries.

"Jess, I told Victoria last night that I didn't want to step on anyone's toes. Does Sheriff Perez know you're out here?"

Jess led his big gray gelding to a nearby hitching post and loosely tied the reins. While he tossed the left stirrup upon the seat of the saddle and tightened the girth, he answered Seth's question, "Of course. I told him."

"And you told him what we're going to do?"

Jess jerked the stirrup back in place before he looped a water canteen around the saddle horn. "He's aware that you've come home to look into the matter of Noah Rider." The undersheriff looked at Seth. "And frankly, he welcomes your help, Seth. We're not exactly bogged down with homicides around here. In fact, they rarely occur. A few manslaughter cases from time to time, but nothing this cryptic. He understands you have years of experience with this type of thing and he also knows you won't do anything that might compromise the case."

Seth felt both flattered and relieved. The last thing he wanted to do was push his nose into a place where he wasn't welcome. "I'm relieved, and I'll try not to make a nuisance of myself."

Chuckling, Jess shook his head. "If you only knew. Seth, the whole department is buzzing about having a Texas Ranger in the area. They see you as some mystical hero and they'd all like to meet you, they're just too afraid to invite you to the office."

Seth laughed with disbelief as he propped his boot on the hitching rail and strapped on a gal-leg spur. "Jess, believe me, there's nothing special about me. I'm just a lawman, that's all. Just a Texas Ranger."

"Yeah," Jess countered with mocking admiration. "You're just a member of the oldest, most elite organization of lawmen in the United States. Hell, the Texas Rangers are even older than the Royal Canadian Mounted Police. You originated back in 1823, there's only a hundred of you, and it's damn hard to become one of those hundred. You have to be smart, strong and morally upright, among a lot of other things.''

Seth lowered his boot to replace it with the other one. As he strapped on the opposite spur, he said, ''That's all true. But you've got to remember that we're only men. We make mistakes. And we don't solve every case that comes our way.''

''Hmm. You can play modest, Seth, because that's your nature. But you can't fool me. You not only got into the Rangers, you've also moved up the ladder. That's bound to make you feel good.''

Seth did feel good about his job. Becoming a Ranger had been a dream he'd been fortunate enough to fulfill. Yet there were times when he was struck by the fact that his job was all he had in life. Like yesterday, when he'd seen Corrina standing with her son on Rube's front porch. The woman was far from rich and he didn't even know if she had a regular job, but she had someone who needed and loved her. She had someone to come home to.

He glanced at the long, lean sheriff and gave him a wry smile. ''No better than you must feel about being married to one of the most beautiful women in San Juan County.''

Jess chuckled. ''See, I knew you were a smart man.''

The two men finished readying their mounts. Five minutes later they headed away from the ranch in a westerly direction through a flat mesa dotted with yucca, prickly pear and sage.

For three miles, the landscape went unchanged until the mesa narrowed down to overlapping foothills shaded sparsely with piñon and ponderosa pine and a few stunted cottonwoods.

Another mile passed as they began to climb to a

higher elevation. As the trail grew steep and rough, the horses began to sweat and blow. Eventually they entered a dry wash with a graveled, rock-strewn bottom. Clear pools of water had collected in dished-out spots of the arroyo. Jess and Seth stopped their horses and allowed the animals to drink their fill.

"What a hell of a place to commit murder," Jess remarked as the two men looked around them.

"Is this the place?" Seth asked.

"Not far. Maybe a hundred more yards on up the arroyo. I'll show you."

Once the horses finished drinking, Seth followed his brother-in-law through the steep, winding gorge. On either side, the tall walls were speckled with huge boulders, clumps of sage and ragged piñon. Here and there a twisted limb of juniper grew tenaciously between slabs of shale.

Seth figured he'd been through this wash before. There wasn't any part of the hundred-thousand-acre ranch that he hadn't seen at least once in his young life. Yet he didn't remember this particular area. Which wasn't all that surprising, considering it had been years since he'd ridden on Ketchum land.

In a matter of minutes, Jess pulled his gray horse to a stop and pointed to a spot in the bed of the wash where two flat rocks formed a vee at the base of a crooked tree trunk.

"This is it," Jess said. "Noah was on those rocks. Facedown. And, as you already know, there was one gunshot wound to his head."

As always when Seth looked at a crime scene, a grim resolution settled over him. "That's a hell of a way to die," he said, his voice rough with emotion. "And I can tell you one thing, Jess, whoever committed the deed is going to pay and pay dearly.''

"I hope you're right, Seth. This murder thing has gotten everybody in the whole county jumpy. And after I was shot—well, we had all kinds of calls coming in to the department from people who were worried about their own safety."

"Where were you and Victoria when that happened?'' Seth asked.

Jess pointed to the ledge of ground far above their head. "Up there. After the bullet hit me, I fell all the way down here. I was unconscious. If Victoria hadn't been with me, I would have quickly bled to death. But with her being a doctor, she knew what to do. And, thank God, she was brave enough to stick around and do it.''

"I couldn't agree more," Seth replied, then shook his head with dismay. "I can't believe one of the T Bar K hands nearly killed you.''

"Steve actually believed he was shooting at Ross, not me. He'd been holding a grudge because Ross wouldn't give him their cousin Linc's job. And then there was that woman, Angela Bowers. Steve wanted her, but she wouldn't have anything to do with him because of Ross.''

Seth's lips twisted ruefully. "Ross always did like the women. In that way he was just like Tucker used to be. And look what it caused. You were nearly killed.''

"Well, to be fair," Jess said, "Ross wasn't having any sort of relationship with Angela. Steve just believed something was going on between them. And that was enough to make him take a potshot at Ross.''

"Thank God Ross quit his playboy ways and married Bella before anyone else got shot around here," Seth exclaimed.

Jess grinned as though the idea of Ross being married still amused him. "Yeah. Ross is a truly converted man now. I never thought I'd see the day." He turned a keen eye on Seth. "So when are we going to hear wedding bells for you, Seth? Haven't you found some Texas beauty you can't live without?"

Seth let out an easy laugh. "Hardly. I'm a busy man. Besides, I'm too set in my ways for any woman to put up with me." And even if he did find one that would be willing to put up with his crazy work schedule, Seth thought, that didn't mean that he would love her or that she would love him.

Love. Seth wasn't even sure he believed in the emotion. Oh, he loved his siblings all right. But that was a different kind of love. He wasn't at all sure that the connection between men and women was anything more than physical lust. As a young boy he'd grown up believing his parents loved each other. That they were married and had children because there was love between them. Later, as a teenager, Seth had realized his father wasn't a devoted husband and his mother was only living a sham of married bliss. The discovery had devastated Seth and opened his eyes to relationships between men and women. And through the years he'd continually vowed to live alone than to live a lie as his parents had done.

"You might be surprised about that," Jess said.

Seth merely smiled at his brother-in-law's response, then motioned for the other man to join him at the vee-shaped rocks.

"Come on, Jess, we've got a little speculating to do."

For the next half hour the two men studied the spot where Noah had been found and discussed the ways in and out of the ranch that the killer might have taken, plus the possible reasons why any of it had happened on the T Bar K.

Eventually, they climbed back on their horses and rode to the ranch. Once there, Jess lingered only a few more minutes before he loaded his big gray gelding and drove away.

With his brother-in-law gone and Ross busy with the cattle, Seth decided he'd use the remainder of the morning to drive into town and make a visit to one of the names on his list.

Montgomery Feed and Grain was located in the older, original part of town and had served the ranchers around Aztec for as long as Seth could remember. The front of the building was made of corrugated iron painted a pale green. Large double doors made of heavy wood stood open to a dark, cavernous interior stacked with tons of feed ranging from wild birdseed to high-protein horse grain. To the right side of the double doors was a high wooden porch connected to the front of the store itself.

As Seth opened a pane-glass door and stepped inside, a cowbell clanged over his head, announcing to the proprietor that a customer had entered the store.

He walked between dusty rows of leather tack, nylon lariats and veterinary supplies until he reached a pine counter rubbed smooth by years of use. Behind it, a gray-haired man with hooded eyes and crinkled, leathery skin rose from a rocking chair and stood to one side of a cash register.

He peered curiously at Seth. "Could I help you?"

Seth leaned against the counter. "Hello, Cal. I'm Seth Ketchum. One of Tucker's sons."

The man planted both hands on the countertop and leaned forward for a closer inspection of Seth. After a moment, a grin split his face. "Why, it sure is you, Seth. Haven't seen you in years, boy. If you hadn't told me, I wouldn't have known you. What are you doing in Aztec? Come up from Texas to investigate the murder?"

At least Cal wasn't going to be evasive, Seth thought wryly. "Not really. The San Juan County Sheriff's Department is handling the case. But if I stumble across any information that might help, I wouldn't turn a deaf ear."

The older man folded his arms across his chest. As he did, Seth couldn't help but notice that the flesh on his arms was flaccid and his shoulders stooped. Cal was somewhat older than what his father would have been if he'd lived, yet it jarred Seth to think Tucker would be as Cal and Rube were now, riddled with arthritis and other geriatric maladies. Up until his heart had given out, Tucker had been so big and vibrant it had been hard to imagine him old or even sick. And even after he'd begun to ail, his presence had remained strong enough to grab everyone's attention.

"I don't blame you," Cal replied. "That was a hell of a thing—Noah getting killed like he did. Tell me, Seth, what kind of lowlife would do such a thing?"

"Criminals come in all shapes and sizes, Cal. If we can figure out the motive, we'll probably find our man. I was wondering if you'd seen Noah recently or talked to him?"

Cal pulled off his John Deere cap and scratched his head. "I guess I haven't seen Noah in—oh, I'd say twenty years or more. He came by here once—that was shortly after he'd quit the T Bar K. Said he was just passing through and wanted to say hello. I didn't know where the man had gotten off to.''

''Can you remember Noah having any enemies around here?''

Cal's forehead wrinkled even more. ''Enemies? Hell no! Everybody liked Noah. Now, your papa was a different matter. Me and Tucker had a few rounds between us. But Noah was a quiet, gentle man who never bothered nobody.''

Seth nodded briefly. ''That's how I remember him, too. And I remember you and Dad having a big row over some feed. Whatever happened about that?''

A grimace twisted the old man's lips. ''I'll tell you what happened. Tucker accused me of selling him moldy horse feed. I didn't. I told him he'd let it get wet then blamed it on me. We went round and round about it. But I finally gave in and shipped three more tons out to the ranch. At no cost. Took me months to make up that loss,'' he added with a huff.

''I can understand you being mad at Dad. But what about Noah? Was he in on any of this argument?''

The old man looked totally surprised by Seth's question. ''Oh, no! It weren't any of Noah's fault. Tucker's the one who let the load get wet.'' He shrugged one shoulder. ''But I forgave your old man for that. He was a good customer over the years. And Ross still buys a lot of feed from me. I'm not offended to take Ketchum money,'' the older man said with a smile.

Seth let out a long breath. ''Well, I'm glad to know you're not harboring any grudge toward Tucker. But I wish you could tell me a little more about Noah,'' Seth admitted.

"I wish I could, too," Cal replied. "You know, it's downright scary to think there might be a killer around here. Most of my customers say they're watchin' their backs. And all of them say they don't ride fence alone. Makes a man wonder what the world is comin' to."

Seth talked a few more minutes with Cal and tried to reassure the older man he believed the killing was an isolated incident and that he shouldn't worry. When he left the feed store, he noticed traffic had picked up on nearby Main Street. Glancing at his watch, he saw that it was approaching the lunch hour.

On sudden impulse, he made a left-hand turn and drove down to the Wagon Wheel Café. If he was lucky, he could get something good to eat and perhaps pick up anything that might be said by the locals about the T Bar K murder. Even though the murder had happened four months ago in early April, he realized the incident was still a source of gossip for the locals.

Moments later, Seth walked into the old diner and instantly felt as though he'd been jetted back in time. Some things never changed, he mused as he looked around at the vinyl booths and long Formica bar with swiveling red stools.

Behind the counter, a waitress was pouring coffee into the cups of the customers lining the bar. Her head was tilted forward, causing a tumble of chestnut curls to hide her face.

Seth took a step toward one of the stools, and then stopped in his tracks as recognition struck him.

Corrina.

Her name shot through his brain at the same time she lifted her head. She spotted him immediately and as their gazes clashed, Seth watched her lips part with surprise, her eyes widen. Something warm and mushy hit him in the stomach.

As he slung a leg over the nearest stool, the feeling spread upward, and by the time she came to stand across from him, he'd figured out the warmth pumping through him was pleasure. And the reason for it was Corrina.

Chapter Three

"Hello, Seth."

Her low, melodious voice filtered through the clatter of dishes and the hum of conversation filling the diner. The sound touched him and sweetened the joy he felt at seeing her again.

"Hello, Corrina."

Their eyes remained locked and an awkward moment of silence passed between them before Corrina finally gave him a brief smile.

"I'm...surprised to see you here." As soon as the words passed his lips, he realized he'd said the same thing yesterday when he'd found her standing on Rube's porch. She probably thought he sounded like a parrot capable of repeating only one phrase.

"Normally I work at the high school as a teacher's aide," she explained. "But since school is out for the summer, I took this job for a little extra income. I was off yesterday when you came out to the ranch."

No wonder she'd looked so tired yesterday, he thought. When she wasn't at home waiting on her father, she was here working on her feet, for God only knew how many hours. Evidently she needed all the income she could get.

"That's good. I mean, good that you were able to find part-time work."

Hell, he silently cursed at himself, what was he doing stuttering along like some tongue-tied teenager? Communicating with people was a major part of his job. He was normally adept at it. But there was something about this woman that made words of any sort seem trite.

She glanced down the bar to where several men were eating the midday meal. Seth took the moment to let his gaze wander over the fiery curls tucked behind her ears, the soft golden-pink blush on her cheekbones and the smooth moist curves of her lips. She was wearing the same uniform as the other waitresses in the diner, a pale pink smock over black slacks. The collar and lapel folded back to expose the column of her throat and an area of skin just beneath. It was creamy white and as fine and smooth as an Egyptian-cotton sheet.

"Are you here for lunch or just something to drink?" she asked.

Her question jerked Seth back to the moment at hand and reminded him that she didn't have time to linger, even if he wanted her to.

"I'll have a hamburger and a cup of coffee," he told her.

She scribbled his request on a notepad in her hand. "It'll take a few minutes," she warned. "We're rather busy today."

"That's fine. I'm in no hurry."

She gave him a grateful smile. "I'll turn this in and get your coffee."

Seth watched her go over to the tall, open counter that separated the working kitchen from the diner itself. A clothesline was strung from one side of the opening to the other. Corrina hurriedly pinned the order to the small white rope with a clothespin, then went to the restaurant-size coffee urn and filled a small, thick-lipped cup.

She carried it and a handful of tiny half-and-half containers back to the spot where he was sitting and placed everything in front of him.

"Thank you, Corrina."

Nodding, she started to move away. Without thinking, he swiped a hand at her forearm to stop her, but missed. However, his action caught her attention and she paused, her eyebrows arched in question as she looked at him.

Seth felt a dull flush of heat creep up his neck. He didn't know why he'd reached out for her like that instead of simply asking her to wait a moment. But his mind didn't seem to work logically when he was in this woman's presence.

"I just…wanted to…I'd like to talk to you about something. When do you think you might have a free moment?" he asked.

Her eyes flickered with speculation before she glanced at the tiny watch strapped to her wrist by a black leather band. "I get a fifteen-minute break in an hour."

He nodded. "I'll see you then."

She frowned. "Uh, what is this—"

"Hey, waitress, we need some coffee down here."

The customer's voice alerted Corrina that she'd already spent too much time serving Seth. With a frustrated glance at the Texas Ranger, she said, "I'll talk to you in a while."

Forty-five minutes later most of the noonday diners were heading back to work. Corrina shouldered her way through a swinging door leading into the kitchen. There, she plopped an armload of dirty dishes into a huge stainless-steel sink filled with soapy water.

"Lord, what a rush. My feet are aching!"

The complaint had Corrina turning to see Betty, a fellow waitress, pushing a weary hand through her brassy blond hair.

"It was busy today," Corrina agreed.

"Busy!" she exclaimed. "Honey, that's an understatement if I ever heard one. But I've got a pocketful of tips. I'll be able to buy that dress I've had my eye on for my granddaughter."

Corrina smiled at the woman who had quickly become her friend since she'd begun working here at the Wagon Wheel two months ago. Betty was coarse-featured and a little rough around the edges, but her heart was pure gold. She'd immediately taken Corrina under her wing and helped her with everything from writing orders to dealing with flirtatious customers.

"I'm glad. And I'm sure your granddaughter will really be surprised when her birthday rolls around and she opens your gift."

Betty glanced at the fry cook, who was busy flipping burgers, then edged closer to Corrina and lowered her voice. "Speaking of tips, who was the big spender at the bar?"

Corrina's expression went blank. "Big spender?"

Betty's eyes rolled toward the ceiling. "Yeah, the one who left you the big bill. The guy in the cream-colored Stetson and burgundy striped shirt. Every woman in the place was looking at him. I've never seen him around here before. But he sure was eyeing you like he knew you pretty well."

Corrina released a pent-up breath. "Oh. That was Seth Ketchum. We…uh…went to high school together. A long time ago. He just happened to remember me."

Betty's wide mouth tilted to a suggestive grin. "Must be nice havin' a man like that remember you. Is he one of those rich Ketchums? The ones that had that murder out on the T Bar K?"

Corrina nodded. "Yes. Seth is one of the Ketchum sons. He's a Texas Ranger."

Betty's eyebrows arched, her eyes popped wide. To say the woman looked impressed by this news was putting it mildly. "I knew he was a Texan!" Betty exclaimed. "Just had that look about him. You know, the kind that makes you stop and stare when he comes into a room."

Corrina could have told the woman that Texas hadn't done that to Seth, it was his own natural presence that drew a person's attention. But at that moment the cook motioned to Betty that her order was ready and the waitress turned away to fetch the plates of burgers and fries.

Corrina followed Betty out of the kitchen and into the restaurant. The bar was empty and the only customers that remained from the earlier rush were seated on the side of the diner that was Betty's responsibility.

Seth had eaten his burger and departed the diner while she'd been busy scurrying from table to table. One minute he'd been seated at the bar and the next minute she'd turned around to find him gone. The tip she'd found by his plate had been so large she was actually embarrassed to stuff it into the pocket on her smock. But she had. Because she needed the money. And because she understood that Seth wanted her to have it.

Yet the generous tip didn't make up for the fact that he'd left without speaking to her, and she had to admit she was feeling a little deflated by his behavior. Especially after he'd made a point of telling her he wanted to talk to her.

Well, none of it mattered, she told herself as she walked from booth to booth straightening napkin holders and salt and pepper shakers. She didn't need to be talking to Seth Ketchum. She didn't need to be thinking of him either. He was not the sort of man who would fit into her life at all. Besides, he was only here for a short duration before he'd be heading back to Texas.

The bell over the door jingled and she looked up thinking it was one of Betty's customers leaving. Instead, her heart skipped an odd little beat as she spotted Seth walking through the door.

She remained standing by the booth and waited for him to approach her. As she watched him stride toward her, she could feel every nerve in her body stand on its head and sizzle with anticipation. By the time he reached her, she was shaking inside and the lopsided smile he was giving her didn't help to soothe her sudden trembles.

"Has your break started yet?" he asked.

Trying to breathe normally, Corrina glanced at her watch. "It's starting now. Would you like more coffee, or iced tea?"

"More coffee might be nice. But only if you're having some," he told her.

"Why don't you sit down," she suggested, gesturing a hand toward the booth. "I'll be right back."

Behind the bar, she quickly gathered two cups of coffee and creamers. As she carried the lot over to the booth, she spotted Betty watching her with undisguised speculation. No doubt her friend was wondering what a well-to-do man like Seth would be doing spending more than a passing moment with a woman like Corrina. Actually, she was wondering that herself. But as she joined him in the booth she tried to act as though having coffee with a Texas Ranger was nothing out of the ordinary, that having a handsome, sexy man seek out her company was just a normal part of her day.

"Is this where you usually take your breaks?" he asked. "I mean, if you had plans to leave the diner, don't let me stop you."

Corrina quickly waved a dismissive hand. "Oh no. Fifteen minutes isn't enough time to run an errand or anything. I usually just sit and try to rest my feet." She stirred cream into her coffee while she berated herself for not taking a moment to powder her nose and dab a bit of color onto her lips. After six hours of work, she knew she looked as washed out as an old dishrag. But then there wasn't any point in trying to impress Seth. He knew what kind of background she'd come from, a place he would never personally know. "Actually, I didn't expect you back," she admitted.

Amusement crinkled his features. "Why not? When I tell someone I'm going to do something, I do it."

Yes, Corrina was quite certain he was a man who stuck to his word and his principles. He wouldn't give a woman false promises the way Dale had done the two years they'd been married. What would it be like, she wondered, to have a relationship with a man who didn't lie to his spouse or think only of himself? A man like Seth?

Embarrassed by her wandering thoughts, she cleared her throat then quickly sipped her coffee. "So…what did you want to talk to me about?" she asked, deciding to get straight to the point.

She could feel his gaze sliding over her skin and hair like an inquisitive hand. The sensation left her hot and cold at the same time.

He said, "I wanted to talk to you about Matthew."

Her son's name was probably the last thing she'd been expecting him to say, and the surprise must have shown on her face because he chuckled as she scooted to the edge of her seat and leaned toward him.

"What did he do?" she asked in a desperate rush beneath her breath. "Did he…insult you yesterday?"

"No," he said with an easy smile. "Your son was very mannerly. I enjoyed spending a few minutes with him, in fact."

Corrina released a breath of relief. "Oh. I'm glad. I—I've tried to raise him right, Seth. But it's not always easy by myself. Sometimes I never know what might come out of his mouth or what he might do. He's an adventurous boy and he needs a male figure in his life. More than just Dad. But…well—" She bent her head and focused her blue eyes on the swirling coffee. "Dale has been out of our lives since Matthew was a toddler. He never sees his son. And I…well, it's probably obvious to you that I never remarried."

He continued to study her face as he wondered what her life had been like since she'd grown into a woman. It couldn't have been easy. Not with raising a son alone and now taking care of an alcoholic father.

The urge to console her had him wanting to reach

across the table and press her hand between the two of his. He wanted to tell her that the world wasn't all gray. That one day her sky would be bright and blue.

"Have you wanted to remarry?"

Her head jerked upward as though she'd been shot. "No!" she uttered forcefully, then floundered as her cheekbones turned scarlet. "I mean, I haven't been looking. Raising Matthew is more important than me having another relationship with a man."

Did she know just how revealing her words were? he wondered. Since she'd been in the same class as Ross, he knew she had to be around thirty-five, yet she was a woman who'd given up on men and marriage. And love. But then that shouldn't be so surprising to a man who'd never gotten remotely close to starting a family.

She touched fingertips to the furrows in her forehead. "I'm sorry, Seth. I didn't mean to run off with the conversation. It's just that—" She broke off, her smile rueful. "It's not too often I have anyone to…lend me an ear."

Suddenly there were so many things he wanted to ask her, to learn about her, but her break was almost over. He couldn't expect her to sit here and loaf away the remainder of the afternoon. Besides, he didn't need to know things about Corrina Dawson. The more he learned about her, the more he would eventually have to forget once he went back home to Texas and resumed his life.

Circling his coffee cup with both hands, he watched the tip of her forefinger move from her forehead down to her lower lip, where it rubbed back and forth against the plush, moist curve. Even though the action was totally innocent on her part, the sensual movement caused a gnawing need to start deep in his belly.

Shocked by the unexpected reaction in his body, he focused his eyes on the brown liquid in his cup. "I'm glad you brought up the subject of Matthew needing male attention. Because I'd like to take him horseback riding. I tossed the idea at him yesterday and he seemed interested. So I promised him I'd talk to you about it. I'd planned on calling you, but after I ran into you here…I thought talking with you face-to-face would be better."

Her heart thudding heavily, Corrina stared at him as all sorts of questions plowed through her mind. The main one being, why would he bother with *her* son?

"Uh…look, Seth, I understand you're busy with Noah's murder case. You couldn't have time to waste on Matthew."

His hazel eyes locked with the blue depths of hers. "It wouldn't be a waste. At least, not for me."

Her chest winced as a mixture of unexpected emotions hit her. "But you…"

Shaking his head, he said, "Corrina, I promised Ross I would do what I could and I will. But that doesn't mean I intend to work every minute of the day."

Corrina didn't know what to think. To be honest, she was totally floored by Seth's suggestion. He'd only met Matthew yesterday and he'd not seen or talked to her in years, close to twenty at least. And even then, the two of them had been casual acquaintances.

Only because you wouldn't let him be more.

The little voice going off in her head shook her, reminded her of a time when she'd dreamed about being someone special to this man, when her young heart had been filled with love for him. Yet she'd never acted on her feelings. She'd only been a teenager at the time, but she'd been mature enough to know a Dawson couldn't rub shoulders with a Ketchum. It would have never worked. Especially while Tucker had been alive. Seth's father had wanted the best for his offspring. And Rube Dawson's daughter wouldn't have made the grade.

"In that case, I'm sure Matthew would love to go riding with you."

He smiled and Corrina realized the easy sign of pleasure on his face was not something she'd seen much of since he'd come to the house yesterday. The notion made her wonder if he was carrying a heavy weight on his shoulders over the Rider case or if something had happened in his past to mute his joy for living.

"Then you have no objection?" he asked.

She laughed softly. "I'm sure if I made objections my son would never speak to me again. But why would I? If he isn't safe with you, he isn't safe with anyone."

He'd had high-ranking political officers in Texas rely on him to protect their very lives, yet to know Corrina trusted her son in his care touched him in a far deeper way. In fact, the pride he was feeling at this moment was downright ridiculous.

"Good. If he's not doing anything tomorrow afternoon about one, I'll drive over and pick him and his horse up and take them back to the T Bar K."

Her eyebrows lifted. "You're going to ride at the Ketchum place?"

He nodded. "Why? Is something wrong?"

She shrugged one shoulder. "Not really. I just assumed you'd be riding on Dad's place."

Her eyes traveled over his face and he could see she was trying her best to size up his motives. Seth could have told her that she was wasting her time. He wasn't even sure himself as to why he was going to this much trouble to show Matthew a little attention. Except that he'd seen a hungry need in the boy's eyes and had wanted, in some way, to try to ease it.

"And you're going to a lot of trouble to go over and pick up his horse," she added.

"I think Matthew will enjoy seeing the ranch," Seth said, deciding it wouldn't be polite to add that he believed the boy needed to get off the Dawson place for a while.

A smile lifted the corners of her lips and her blue eyes twinkled at the thought of how much pleasure her son was going to derive from this outing with Seth. "He'll probably stay awake tonight just waiting for you to show up."

"I have a nine-year-old nephew, Aaron. He's my late brother's son. I might include him on the ride, too. If it's okay with his mother, Maggie. After Hugh was gored to death by a bull, she's a little hesitant about letting her son get around horses or cattle. But she doesn't forbid it and I think she'll agree. If that's all right with you."

Over his shoulder, Corrina spotted the manager of the diner coming out of the kitchen. A quick glance at her watch told her she'd already gone two minutes over her break. Not wanting to jeopardize her job, she rose to her feet and picked up her dirty coffee cup.

"Of course it's all right. I'll tell Matthew to be ready tomorrow. Right now, I've got to get back to work." As she turned away from the booth, she shot him a grateful smile. "Thank you, Seth."

Early the next morning, Seth stood on the front porch and kissed his new sister-in-law's cheek. A step away, Ross looked on with an indulgent glare.

"Here now," he warned. "That's as far as you go, Tex."

Isabella smiled daintily at her brother-in-law. "Good-bye, Seth. Take care of yourself while we're gone," she urged him.

"I will," Seth assured her, then to his brother he said, "Don't be so greedy, brother. You're going to have your pretty wife all to yourself for the next two weeks."

Grinning, Ross reached for his wife and, with both hands around her rib cage, lifted her off her feet. "Yeah, and I can't wait," he said. "Ready to go, honey?"

Ross's darker-skinned, half-Apache wife smiled adoringly down at her husband. "I'm very ready."

The intense love on Bella's face was like nothing Seth had ever seen. And though he wasn't in the market for a wife, he couldn't but help feel an empty loss and a ridiculous sense of envy.

Setting her back on her feet, Ross curled his arm around Isabella's waist and urged her toward the waiting pickup truck where their luggage was already loaded.

Sauntering after them, Seth waited until they'd climbed inside the cab before he stuck his nose in the open window. "It's not bothering you one little bit to go off and leave me all alone, is it?"

Ross laughed. "It's not my fault you're alone."

No, it was his own choice, Seth thought. But there were times like this one when he wondered if his life would ever change. Moreover, did he really want it to? He could go and do as he pleased. He didn't have to answer to anyone. And the only person he had to take care of was himself. All those things outweighed the loneliness he sometimes felt. Didn't it?

"Well, you two enjoy the Caribbean," he said.

"We will," Ross assured him with a grin, then just as quickly the grin was replaced with concern. "Just be sure and watch your back, brother. I don't want anything to happen to you while we're gone. Or anytime, for that matter."

Seth frowned. "Are you forgetting Steve Chambers is behind bars?"

"Yeah, Steve tried to kill me. But someone *did* kill Noah. And he's still out there on the loose."

Seth reached through the window and squeezed Ross's shoulder. "Don't go off on your honeymoon thinking about any of that, Ross. Linc is here with me. We'll keep things going and we'll be safe. Promise."

Seemingly satisfied that Seth and their cousin could keep things running smoothly and safely, Ross said a final goodbye and started the truck.

Seth waved them off and then watched as the vehicle made its way down the hill, past the ranch yard, the barns, and finally the bunkhouse. Once it was out of sight, he walked back into the kitchen and found Marina sitting at the table dabbing her eyes with the corner of her apron.

"Well, if this isn't something," he scolded softly. "You're sitting here boohooing over Ross being gone. Don't I count for anything?"

Marina blew her nose, then sniffed. "'Course you count. But I'm used to you being gone. It's always awful quiet when Ross is away."

Seth patted the woman's shoulder. "The days will pass before you notice. Besides, I'll try to give you as much trouble as I can so you'll think Ross is still around."

Marina snorted, then chuckled, then looked at him and smiled. "I didn't know you could make a joke."

"There's a lot you don't know about me," he said as he walked over to the counter and poured himself a cup of coffee. "I guess that's my fault though. I should have been coming back home on a regular basis."

"You have important work to do, Seth. We understand that. And we're all very proud of you."

Seth turned a grateful eye her way. "I know. But sometimes I miss being around my family."

Twisting her head around, Marina leveled a stern look on him. "You've lived alone too long. If your mother was still alive, she'd be very unhappy about that."

Seth grimaced. "Don't go using that tactic on me, Marina. Mother always understood the choices I made. Much more than Dad ever did. She knew that I would never marry just for the sake of having a wife or kids. If there is such a thing as love, I want to find it. I don't want things to be—" He broke off, uncertain about how much he could say to this woman without upsetting her. Even though he had a feeling that Marina knew private things about his parents' marriage, she'd never spoken of the problems between Tucker and Amelia. Probably because she had loved both of them equally. Just as Seth had. "I don't want things to be forced," he finally finished. "I'd rather be alone than live that way."

Rising from her chair, Marina began to gather the dirty dishes from the table. "Sometimes it's not meant for a person to find love. Sometimes a person has to settle for less."

"Not me." He tossed back the last of his coffee and placed his cup in the sink just as Marina approached with an armload of plates. "I'm going to drive up to the Double X this morning, Marina. But I'll be back by lunch. I was wondering if you could fix a few snacks for my saddlebags. I'm taking Aaron and another boy riding this afternoon. They might get hungry.''

Always glad to be needed, she gave him a bright smile. ''I'll fix 'em right up. No little boys will ever go hungry around here,'' she said, then her eyes narrowed on him. ''What you going up to the Double X for? That's an hour away from here.''

''I'm going to talk to James, see if he'd been in touch with Noah at any time before he was killed. I'm sure they were once friends. James purchased a lot of cattle from Dad during those days that Noah was foreman.''

''Why don't you just call him?'' Marina suggested.

One corner of Seth's mouth lifted as he shook his head. ''You can't question a person over the phone, Marina. You have to look them in the eye, watch their reactions to see if they're telling the truth or if anything else is going on with them.''

She dropped the plates into the soapy water. ''Well, you've went a little loco if you suspect James Miller of killing Noah! That man is a—well, he's a saint!''

''Even saints sometimes fall from grace, Marina. And when they do, it's my job to expose them,'' he said.

With troubled eyes, Marina watched him walk out of the kitchen.

Seth spent most of the morning talking with James Miller, owner of the Double X. The property was just a tad smaller than the T Bar K, but unlike the Ketchum ranch, it didn't raise horses. And all of its cattle was sold directly to feedlots for meat and by-products rather than sold to other ranchers for breeding purposes.

Like his late father, James had aged. Yet the tall,

rawboned man had greeted Seth with a firm grip and a sincere warmth that couldn't be faked. It was quickly obvious to Seth that the saint hadn't fallen. And he'd spent the remainder of the morning simply visiting with an old friend. Unfortunately, James hadn't seen or heard from Noah Rider and, just as Seth and his family, he'd been shocked to hear of the old foreman's death.

One by one Seth was checking off the names on his list and so far the interviews had produced nothing in the way of clues. But that was nothing new in detective work. He'd investigated many cases where it appeared there were absolutely no leads or hope of finding one, when suddenly a break would come right out of the blue and facts would begin to fall into place. Seth could only hope something along that order would eventually happen in the matter of Noah's murder.

One thing was for certain, he thought as he pulled back into the T Bar K ranch yard. He didn't want to head back to Texas with the case unsolved. It wasn't in his nature to quit on a thing. Yet he couldn't stay in New Mexico indefinitely. He had four weeks' leave from his job and one of those was nearly gone. Once his leave was over, his superior would be expecting him back on the job.

As Seth headed to the horse barn to saddle Juggler, he did his best to push the whole problem out of his mind. This afternoon was going to be for his nephew and for Matthew Dawson. Although, he was beginning to ask himself if getting involved with Corrina's son was a wise thing on his part. Yesterday in the diner he'd been strongly attracted to her. Hell, it had been more than attraction, he'd been mesmerized by everything about her. A little more time around the woman and he'd probably be besotted with her. And that would never do. He'd always made it a point of steering clear of relationships he knew would never work. And Corrina had made it clear she wasn't looking to have a man in her life.

An hour later, Seth arrived on the Dawson place. Matthew was standing out in the driveway waiting for him. The boy was dressed in jeans and boots and a black crumpled hat with a crease down the middle of the crown such as the old western movie stars had worn. The youngster's eagerness put a grin on Seth's face.

"I wasn't sure whether you wanted me to have Blackjack saddled or not. So I didn't saddle him. But I have everything ready," Matthew said in a rush of excitement.

Seth smiled at the boy and as he did, all his earlier doubts about seeing Corrina's son faded away. If he could give this child just an afternoon of enjoyment, it would be worth the effort.

"That's good," he told Matthew. "I'd rather haul a horse unsaddled. We'll put the saddle and the rest of the tack in the saddle compartment in the trailer."

The two of them headed to the corral to collect Blackjack. Matthew skipped alongside Seth's long strides.

"Does Aaron get to come too?" the boy asked. "I sure hope so! He's always nice to me. Ya know, he don't ever act like he's rich."

Because Maggie was doing a bang-up job of raising him, Seth thought. To Matthew he said, "Aaron doesn't live like a rich kid. In fact, he's a lot like you. He doesn't have a father. And he doesn't live in town where he could have plenty of buddies to hang out with. He's pretty much alone, too."

Matthew scuffed the toe of his worn boot against the red ground. "Yeah, but there's plenty of things going on at the T Bar K. Pa says there're lots of cowboys there and even a real bunkhouse! There's nothin' around here."

The two of them had reached the corral where Blackjack was haltered and tied to the fence. While Matthew dealt with the horse's lead rope, Seth said, "Maybe you can change that someday, Matthew. When my father and his brother started the T Bar K, there was nothing there. And they had very little money between them. But they were smart and they worked hard. You could do the same with this place, once you become a man and set your mind to it."

Matthew paused and looked at him with wide, wondrous eyes. "You really think so?"

"I wouldn't say anything I didn't mean."

A broad grin settled over Matthew's face and Seth might have imagined it, but he thought the boy's shoulders straightened just a bit taller.

"Boy, that would be something! Wouldn't Mom be proud?"

Seth patted the boy's back. "I have a feeling your mother is already proud, Matthew."

Matthew looked up at him, his young features squinched against the bright afternoon sun. "Do you have any kids, Seth?"

A wry smile briefly touched Seth's face. "No. Why?"

"'Cause it sure would be nice to have a daddy like you."

A daddy like you.

The words were so simple, yet Seth felt his chest fill

with unexplainable warmth, his throat tighten with an emotion he didn't understand.

For long moments he couldn't speak and then when he could, he had no idea what to say. What did a man say to a child who'd been deserted by his father? What did he say to a young boy who was looking at him as if he was a hero?

Deciding it would be best to keep things light, he placed his hand on the back of Matthew's neck and gave the boy's head an affectionate shake.

"I'm honored that you feel that way, Matthew. But I'll bet you that someday your mother is going to give you a daddy that will be much better than I ever could be at the job."

Matthew grimaced as only a child could. "I ain't gonna hold my breath 'til that happens."

Seth chuckled. "You *aren't* going to hold your breath," he corrected the boy, then nudged him forward. "Come on, let's go to the T Bar K. We have some riding to do."

And he had some thinking to do. Not about Noah Rider's murder. No, this was much more personal, Seth realized. He needed to figure out why he couldn't get Corrina Dawson out of his head and why just seeing her again was making him feel like a different man. A man he'd never met before.

Chapter Four

Once Seth and Matthew reached the T Bar K they saddled their horses under the watchful eye of the oldest wrangler on the ranch. He was a razor-thin man with grizzled whiskers and two hawk feathers stuck in the brim of his gray hat. His name was simply Skinny and he'd worked longer than any hand on the ranch, barring Marina. He'd never had a family, but he took to children like ducks to water and they did the same to him. In a matter of five minutes, he had Matthew enthralled with a story of hunting wild horses in Nevada.

"We'd better be going, Matthew," Seth spoke up, then looked at the old wrangler. "This boy is missing something, Skinny. Do you think we could find him some spurs?"

Skinny looked down at the bare heels of Matthew's brown boots. "Well darned if you ain't right, Seth. A range rider can't go off without his spurs."

Skinny turned and headed into the horse barn while Matthew glanced wide-eyed at Seth. "Is he going for a pair of spurs for me?"

There was such an incredulous tone to Matthew's voice that Seth couldn't help but feel a pang of sadness. Obviously Matthew wasn't accustomed to receiving gifts. Even worse, his attitude implied that he wasn't at all sure he deserved anything given to him.

"Sure is."

"You mean I'm just gonna borrow them?"

With a soft chuckle, Seth patted Matthew on the arm. "My brother is always griping about the tack room being full of junk. He'll be happy to get rid of a pair of spurs. In fact, I'll bet we can find a pair of chaps, too. Would you like to go look?"

For a moment Matthew looked as though he was going to burst with excitement. Finally, his mouth fell open. "Boy, would I!"

Minutes later they left the ranch with Matthew proudly donning his spurs and chaps. Seth didn't bother asking himself if he was doing all of this for Matthew because he was Corrina's child. The reason didn't matter. Just seeing the joy on the boy's face lifted Seth's spirits and he realized seeing the world through a youngster's eyes made a man appreciate the simple blessing of waking up every day.

Five minutes later they had traveled on up the graveled ranch road to where Maggie Ketchum and her son, Aaron, lived. Seth's nine-year-old nephew already had his horse saddled and was waiting by the front gate for Matthew and his uncle to arrive. Maggie was waiting with him and Seth's heart winced as he looked at her lovely face. Hugh's red-haired widow was a beautiful woman who was trying her best to break away from the grief of the past, yet the dullness in her eyes told Seth she hadn't made much headway.

Rusty-haired, freckle-faced Aaron was two years younger than Matthew, but what he lacked in age, he made up for in enthusiasm. As soon as he spotted his uncle and Matthew approaching, he leaped on his horse and spurred him through the gate with a loud "Yippee ti yi ay!"

Maggie yelled at her spirited son. "Aaron! You're going to break your neck! Pull up that horse! Or you're not going anywhere!"

Apparently not wanting to peeve his mother further, the boy pulled the horse to a rapid halt. "Oh, Mom, I wasn't hurtin' nothin'," he said with a groan.

Maggie looked at Seth and helplessly rolled her eyes. "Please make him mind, Seth. And don't let him gallop. There are too many gopher holes out there for him to step in."

Seth smiled patiently at his sister-in-law. "Don't worry, Maggie. I'm going to take them up in the mountains. They'll have to ride slowly and in single file." He glanced at his watch. "So don't expect us back for three or four hours."

With a nod that she understood, she waved them off and Seth and the two boys headed their horses toward the east and the high-desert mountains.

By late that evening Aaron and Matthew had lost some of their energy, but they weren't quite ready to part company for the day. The moment they rode into the ranch yard, Aaron began begging his uncle to allow Matthew to stay for supper.

"Marina is cooking barbacoa. I've already asked

her,'' Aaron informed Seth. ''And Mom won't care if I eat with you tonight.''

Maggie was lenient about letting Aaron spend time with his uncles and the men who worked for the T Bar K, especially while school was out during the summer months. But he had no idea what Corrina would say about the matter.

Seth looked at Matthew. ''Would you like to stay?''

Matthew's expression was suddenly torn. ''Yeah. But Mom will be expecting me home soon. She'll be worried if I don't show up.''

''We could call her,'' Seth suggested.

Aaron and Matthew shouted in unison. ''Yeah! Yeah!''

''Okay. You two boys unsaddle your horses while I go use the telephone. And make sure you brush them down and water them.''

Rather than walking all the way back to the house, Seth dismounted and went inside the horse barn where a phone and a directory were fastened to the wall of the tack room. In a matter of moments, he'd found the Dawson number and heard Corrina's soft voice on the other end of the line.

''Corrina, it's me, Seth.''

There was a moment's pause, then she said, ''Oh. Is—is anything wrong, Seth?''

''No. Everything is fine. We're back from our ride and the boys are tending to their horses. I'm calling to see if you'd like to come have supper with us. The boys want to eat together and they've been having such a good time, I hated to tell them no.''

Corrina breathed deeply. Never in her wildest imaginings had she ever expected to be invited to the

T Bar K. Just the thought of it made her shake with nerves. Or was it Seth who was doing that to her? Either way, the disturbance going on inside her couldn't be good.

"I—I don't have any problem with Matthew staying for supper. And it's very nice of you to invite him. But I'd…better decline. I have lots of things to do tonight."

Like fetch and carry for your lazy father, Seth thought, then frowned. That wasn't quite fair to Corrina, he decided. Rube might not be a candidate for father of the year, but he was obviously important to Corrina. "I'm glad you've given your son permission to stay. But don't you think it would be extra nice for him to have his mother here with him?"

It was true that she and Matthew didn't get to have very many outings together. And having supper at the T Bar K was an opportunity that wouldn't be repeated. But would it be wise to accept his invitation? After all, she'd carried a torch for the middle Ketchum son for twenty years now. She didn't want to do anything to make that torch burst into flame. Not when she knew a relationship with him could only be temporary.

"It's very nice of you, but—"

"No buts," he interrupted. "You don't want to disappoint Matthew." *Or me,* he wanted to add.

The last thing she wanted to do was disappoint her son. He'd had too many of those in his young life already.

"All right," she conceded with a sigh. "I'll change clothes and drive over. It'll take me about twenty minutes."

"No," he quickly replied. "Don't bother driving. I have to bring Matthew's horse home anyway. I'll pick you up at the same time."

Certain she wouldn't win if she tried to argue with him, she agreed to be ready and hung up the phone. Across the room, her father studied her with a troubled expression.

"Who was that?"

"Seth. He's invited me and Matthew to have supper on the T Bar K."

A wide grin split Rube's face. "Well now, see there, honey, I told you years ago that you should have went after the boy. He's the best one of the Ketchums. The least like his daddy. He'd be a good catch for my little pumpkin."

Corrina's face grew warm. Sometimes her father could be so crass she wanted to yell at him. But being disrespectful wasn't in her. And not for anything did she want to deliberately hurt him.

Rising to her feet, she said, "Dad, Seth isn't interested in me that way. And I would never think of *any* man as a catch!"

"Aw now, honey, don't get all fired up just 'cause your old daddy used the wrong words. I just meant Seth'd make a good husband. God knows the other one you had was a born loser. But you got in a hurry when you married Dale. You just saw the little good in him instead of all the bad. I'm hopin' you won't make that mistake the next time."

"Believe me, Dad, there won't be any *next time*," Corrina muttered as she hurried out of the room.

Fifteen minutes later she was dressed in a white-and-yellow gingham blouse with three-quarter-length sleeves and a boat neck collar that exposed the smooth, pale column of her throat. Her straight skirt was white sheeting with short slits on both sides. The outfit was cool, comfortable and feminine. And hopefully nice enough to pass muster for a simple supper. If Seth was expecting anything fancy, he'd be disappointed, because she didn't own anything fancy.

He arrived only moments after she stepped from her bedroom, and after a quick goodbye to her father, she walked outside to see him returning from the barn.

"You've already put Blackjack up in the corral?" she asked.

He smiled at the beautiful picture she made standing in the evening twilight, the blaze of curls around her head tinged with the last pink rays of sunset.

"There's nothing slow about me," he said and then swept her with a pointed look. "You look lovely. Are you ready to go?"

Lovely. Seth Ketchum thought *she* looked lovely. The idea thrilled every womanly particle inside of her. But the practical side of her figured the compliment was just his way of being mannerly.

She nodded to his question. "Yes. But I think I should drive my car anyway. After supper, Matthew and I will need a way to get back home," she reminded him.

With a faint smile, he placed his hand against the small of her back and urged her toward his waiting truck. The casual touch was like an electrical jolt to her system. For a moment it stopped her breath and caused her heart to skip several beats.

"I'll drive you two back," he said, totally unaware of the chaos he was creating in her. "Quit worrying."

Biting her lip, she sternly reminded herself to get a grip. Seth was nothing more than just an old friend. That's the way he saw her and that's the way she had to think of him.

"But it's ten miles from here to your ranch," she

argued. "And you've already made two round trips over here today!"

"That's nothing. I have to commute thirty miles one way to work every day. Besides, the drive between here and the T Bar K is a pretty one. And it gives me time to think."

She glanced at him curiously. "You need that? Time to think?"

One corner of his mouth lifted slightly. "I have a lot in my head to sort out."

"About Noah's murder?"

He opened the passenger door on the truck and helped her up into a bucket seat upholstered in butter-soft leather. "Mostly," he answered.

Smoothing down her skirt, she watched him walk around the hood of the truck, then climb in beside her and start the engine. Any other time, Corrina would have considered the cab of the truck roomy, but with Seth sitting only a few inches away, she felt as though the two of them were cocooned in a quiet, dark place. And she foolishly wondered if he could hear her quickened breathing or the labored pounding of her heart.

As she strapped on her seat belt, she cast a few surreptitious glances in his direction. He was obviously still wearing the clothes he'd worn riding. A blue denim shirt with pearl snaps covered his broad shoulders. Faded blue jeans stretched across his muscled thighs and down the long length of his legs. Spurs were still strapped to his boots, and instead of the cream-colored Stetson he'd worn into the Wagon Wheel, a black hat covered with red dust was settled low on his forehead. He wore the cowboy trappings with ease, but then he should, Corrina thought. He'd been raised the son of a rancher and she suspected that lifestyle hadn't changed, even though he'd moved to Texas and become a lawman.

"How did the ride go?" she asked, hoping to mask her nervousness with conversation.

Seth turned the truck and trailer onto the dirt road that would eventually lead them to a connecting county road. "Couldn't have been better. We rode to the mountains, to a waterfall where I used to go as a boy. I had a saddlebag full of snacks that Marina had prepared, so Matthew and Aaron stuffed themselves. They seemed to love the whole thing. Especially when we spotted a herd of elk."

"That's unusual, isn't it? To see more than one or two elk at a time."

"The cows are down in the foothills now, calving. We were lucky enough to ride near enough to see them."

"Sounds nice," she said, unaware of the wistful tone in her voice. "I can't remember the last time I've been riding. Matt tries to get me on Blackjack, but riding alone isn't nearly as fun."

Fun? Had the woman ever had any fun? Seth wondered. From the weariness he sometimes spotted in her blue eyes, he didn't much think so. Which bothered the hell out of him. He'd always wanted and hoped for Corrina to have a good, happy life. She'd not deserved the hard, hungry years she'd had as a child and teenager. Nor did she deserve the life she was living now.

During their high school years, Seth had often wished he could have talked to her more, given her the support and attention she'd needed. But each time he'd tried, she'd kept a polite wall between them. Now that he was back in New Mexico, he wished that she would, at least, allow him to be her friend.

"Maybe we could go riding," he suggested. "Before I go back to Texas."

Her heartbeat thudded even faster as she glanced at him from beneath her lashes. "Oh, I don't know," she murmured. "I'm out of practice. And I'm very busy."

"Surely you have a day off," he persisted. "You can't work all the time."

Realizing she was twisting her fingers together, she forced her hands to relax in her lap and stared forward rather than at him. The man was simply too potent, too masculine for any normal woman like her to deal with.

"I do have a day off. But I use it to get things done at home. That's the way it is with women who work outside the home."

And women who take on extra responsibilities, he thought. "Well, think about it anyway," he said quietly. "You might decide you can leave some of that work undone." He glanced at her. "Matthew tells me you used to have two horses. And that Rube sold the gray mare not too long ago."

Corrina nodded. "Dad decided it cost too much to feed the both of them."

"Who did he sell her to, do you know?"

A thoughtful frown wrinkled her forehead. "I'm not sure. Why?"

"Oh, I've been looking to buy a good gray mare for my ranch down in Texas. I thought maybe the person might be ready to sell her."

Corrina shrugged. "Well, I think he sold the mare to Cal Montgomery. He owns the feed and grain in town."

Seth nodded. "I know Cal. I'll talk to him before I leave."

Ten minutes later, they turned off the county road and rattled across a wooden cattle guard. Above it, a black pipe formed an arch. In the middle of the arch a piece of black iron had been shaped to the T Bar K brand. It was a simple entrance. Not at all elaborate or showy as some folks had with much smaller properties in the area. But Corrina realized the Ketchums didn't need a huge brick entrance with water fountains and electronic gates. That simple brand was impressive all by itself.

Once on the ranch's property, the road began to climb and soon Corrina could see they were winding close to the river's edge. Since it was nearing August, the snow-melt was mostly over and the depth of the river had sunk to wading level. Black Angus were grazing along the banks and the green meadows beyond.

For several more minutes they traveled upward through pine and juniper and an occasional aspen. When the road topped out, the forest opened up and Corrina found herself looking at the T Bar K ranch yard.

Barns and buildings were numerous and all connected to wooden or metal corrals. The bunkhouse was a long building made of logs, a miniature example of the ranch house itself, which sat farther upon the side of the mountain.

As Seth pulled up to the front-yard gate of the ranch house, he looked over to see Corrina staring all around her.

"What are you thinking?" he asked.

She let out a long breath. "I—I've never seen anything quite like it. I was expecting the house to be different. Sort of like a mansion. But this is even better. It's like a real home."

It had been a real home, Seth thought. Until he'd learned that his father was an adulterer. But years had passed since then and Tucker and Amelia were gone.

The ranch was a different place now that his brother had taken control.

"It is a real home," he told Corrina. "Ross and Bella have made it into one."

"Yes, I heard that Ross had gotten married," she said and then her eyes widened with afterthought. "Oh, I wasn't thinking, are we—Matthew and I—barging in on them? For Pete's sake, newlyweds don't need company!"

Her discomfiture brought a chuckle from Seth. "Don't worry so much, Corrina. Ross and Bella are gone to the Caribbean on their honeymoon. They won't be back for two weeks."

"Oh. That's good. I mean, I wouldn't want to impose on them."

He unbuckled his seat belt and opened the door. "You wouldn't be. The ranch is a big place and Ross likes friends to show up. In fact, Bella is going to want to meet you."

Corrina's hand unconsciously touched her bosom. "Me?"

"Wait right there," he said, then slid out of the truck and went around to open her door. Reaching a hand up to her, he asked, "Why wouldn't Bella want to meet you? You're her neighbor."

Flustered by his question and the fact that he was being such a courtly gentleman, she fumbled with her seat belt then finally managed to push it away from her lap.

"Yes, but—I—well, she's a lawyer."

"So. Lawyers like to have friends, too, just like everybody else."

She rolled her eyes. "Oh, Seth. You're...I think you're blind."

Corrina placed her hand in his and he helped her to the ground. Once she was standing close beside him, he caught her eyes with his and gave her a slow smile.

"No, I think you're the one who's having trouble seeing things." He placed his hand against her back and urged her toward the small wooden gate that opened into the front yard. "Come on, I want you to meet Marina."

As they walked through the enormous house, Corrina didn't notice much about her surroundings, other than the low, beamed ceilings and polished tile floors scattered with rich Navajo rugs. She was too busy trying to ignore the red-hot sensations that Seth's hand was causing to flow through her back. It had been ages since a man had touched her. To have the man of her dreams doing it, even in a casual way, was turning her senses topsy-turvy.

"Here's the kitchen," he announced as they approached a swinging louvered door.

The room was everything a kitchen should be, Corrina thought as she glanced around her. There were plenty of varnished pine cabinets and spacious work counters, heavy-duty appliances and a big pine table with lots of chairs pushed beneath its long length. Nearby the table, a large-pane window shed the late-evening light on several potted succulents.

"Marina, put that spoon down and come here," Seth ordered. "I want you to meet someone."

A large Hispanic woman with graying black hair turned away from an enormous gas range to look at Seth and Corrina.

"Well," she said with an eagle eye on Corrina, "who is this?"

"Her name is Corrina—" Uncertain as to whether

she went by her maiden name now that she was divorced, he glanced at her for help.

Corrina gave the woman a fleeting smile. "Dawson," she finished for him. "I'm Corrina Dawson."

Marina smiled and Corrina felt a sense of relief as she shook the older woman's hand.

"And I'm Marina. The cook and housekeeper and mama around here."

With a faint grin, Seth stepped to Marina's side and planted a kiss on her round cheek. "Us boys would have never gotten grown if it hadn't been for you, Marina. 'Course, I don't know why you had to spoil Ross and ruin him like you did."

Marina gave him a soft whack on the arm. "I not ruin nobody around here," she scolded.

He laughed softly and Corrina could quickly see that Marina definitely held a place in Seth's heart.

"Corrina is going to eat supper with us, Marina. So you make sure you don't burn anything." He winked at Corrina.

The cook waved a hand at him and turned back to the gas range. "Better go get those boys," she warned. "I'm about to dish it all up."

Seth headed to a phone hanging on the kitchen wall. "I'll call down to the barn and tell Skinny to send them on up here," he told Corrina.

In a matter of moments Matthew and Aaron burst through the back door. Both of the boys were out of breath, their faces dirty, their eyes bright with excitement.

"Hi, Mom!" Matthew called to his mother.

"Is it time to eat?" Aaron asked.

"It will be as soon as you two get washed up," Seth

said. "Aaron, you show Matthew where the bathroom is, okay?"

Aaron grabbed his older friend by the arm and urged him out of the kitchen. "C'mon, Matt. We can wash together!"

As soon as they disappeared from sight, running boots could be heard echoing down the hallway.

"Seth, they're running through the house," Corrina exclaimed in horror. "I'll punish Matthew for this."

Smiling, he shook his head. "Don't be silly. It won't hurt this once. They're having a good time and they still have a lot of energy to burn off."

"But they might break something. And Matthew knows the rule of not running indoors," she reasoned, amazed that her son had so quickly made himself at home on this ranch, a place that was far and above anyplace they'd ever lived.

"Rules are sometimes meant to be broken," Seth said.

The indulgent curl to the corner of his lips told Corrina he was enjoying giving the boys a loose rein. Lord help the children he would someday have, she thought. They'd be spoiled rotten.

But then maybe Seth would never marry or have children, her mind went on. He had to be thirty-nine or forty. Maybe he'd decided a long time ago that he wanted to remain a bachelor.

Well, even if he had made that decision, that didn't stop her heart from running a race every time she looked at him. Which only proved that her disastrous marriage to Dale hadn't taught her anything.

Still, it was a sad thing to think a good man like Seth would never be a father. Yet somehow it was even sadder to think of him loving any woman, except her.

Get a hold of yourself, Corrina! You're only having supper with the man and you're lucky to be doing that much.

Thankfully, the ridiculous track of her thoughts was suddenly interrupted as the boys burst back into the kitchen and Seth urged them all to take a seat at the pine table.

"Sit here, Corrina," he said.

He motioned to one corner of the table and she allowed him to help her into the wooden chair, while the two boys scrambled to take seats next to each other on the opposite side of the table. Seth took a chair at the end, just to Corrina's right, and Marina began to serve the barbacoa wrapped in warm flour tortillas, along with the traditional side dishes of refried beans and Spanish rice.

For the first few minutes of the meal Matthew and Aaron were virtually bursting to describe the details of their ride to Corrina. But eventually the conversation turned to the subject of Seth and his being a Texas Ranger.

"Mom, Seth's badge is made from a real Mexican coin," Matthew exclaimed. "Show her, Seth!"

"Your mother doesn't care about seeing my badge," he told Matthew. "That's just something menfolk are interested in."

Corrina arched an eyebrow at him. "Menfolk? Sorry to contradict you, but I'm interested."

Seeing he had no choice in the matter, he dragged the badge from his jeans pocket and placed it in her open palm.

"It's just a badge, Corrina. A lone star in a circle. It's not even shiny, like most law official badges."

Lifting her gaze from the dull piece of silver, she cast

him a wry smile. "A thing doesn't have to glitter to be impressive."

Leaning up in her chair, she reached across the corner of the table and held the star up to the left side of his breast. "Would you pin it on for me?" she asked.

He couldn't have looked more shocked. "Pin it on? But why?"

Corrina supposed she should have been embarrassed for asking such a thing of him. But she wasn't. With a tiny shrug of one shoulder, she said, "Because I've never seen you wear it."

"Corrina—" He broke off self-consciously.

"Seth, this is where you were born and raised. You were my classmate, my neighbor. Not many men around here went on to make something of themselves like you have. I was very proud when I heard you'd become a Ranger."

To hear Corrina Dawson say she was proud of him was enough to make Seth pin the badge on and never take it off. He cast her a wry glance as he pinned the star just above the left pocket on his shirt. "You're making way too much of this, Corrina. But thank you."

She smiled softly at him. "It looks nice, Seth. Real nice."

A lump suddenly thickened his throat and he silently cursed himself for being so sentimental. Hell's bells, he'd been given an award for bravery by the governor of Texas. Plus countless other honors had been bestowed upon him by both local and state officials. Yet none of those accolades had touched him as much as Corrina's simple words.

His gaze was tender as it slipped over her face. "Thank you, Corrina."

"You're welcome," she murmured. Their eyes met

and something in the depth of his pulled on her until the sudden, almost uncontrollable urge to reach over and touch him was so strong, she desperately reached for her fork and shoveled the utensil into her food.

Across the table the boys didn't appear to notice any underlying tension between the two adults and soon their chatter took over the conversation. After a few moments Corrina's lungs began to work on an even keel again, and by the time the meal was nearly finished she'd convinced herself that she'd merely imagined the undercurrent drawing her to Seth.

After all, it had been months since she'd been out with a man. No, correct that, she thought wryly. Years had passed since she'd accompanied a male on any sort of outing, even a platonic meal such as this. She was simply nervous and self-conscious at being out of her element with a well-to-do man like Seth.

"Uncle Seth, can me and Matthew go up to my house and play basketball?" Aaron asked as he swallowed the last bite from his plate.

Seth started to correct his nephew's grammar but just as quickly decided to let it pass this time. He didn't want to be rigid. Not with a nine-year-old boy and not the way Tucker had been. Besides, too many corrections soon began to fall on deaf ears.

"You should be asking Corrina's permission, Aaron," he answered his nephew. "But as far as I'm concerned you may. Just be sure you stay there once you get to your house."

Aaron looked expectantly at Corrina. "Can Matthew go, Ms. Dawson?"

She looked to Seth, who gave her a subtle nod of assurance before she said, "I suppose it will be all right.

But only for a little while. Matthew and I will have to be going home soon.''

''Aw, shoot!'' Aaron groaned.

''Oh, Mom, we just got here,'' Matthew added his protest right behind his buddy's.

''Don't sit there wasting what time you have left with complaining,'' Seth told them. ''You'd better get out of here before Corrina changes her mind.''

The boys didn't wait around to be told a second time. They jumped up from the table and scurried out the back door. As soon as they hit the porch, Corrina and Seth could hear them yipping like wild coyotes.

Seth looked at her and smiled. ''Sounds like they're on their way. There's a little sunlight left, would you like to go out and take a walk on the mesa?''

Marina had left a few minutes earlier for her small house, which Seth had told her was located a short distance down the mountain from here. And the boys would be occupied until dark. Walking on the mesa would definitely be much safer than staying in this quiet house, alone with a man that she'd never quite been able to push out of her heart.

you're simply a nice man or a glutton for punishment," she said.

A quirk of amusement moved his lips. "Why is that?"

"For taking on two boys for the whole afternoon."

He sighed as he looked out over the mesa that stretched for several hundred acres. "I've enjoyed having them with me. They make me think of when Hugh and Ross and I were that age. We had some great adventures here on the ranch. Until we got older and Dad put us to work."

Corrina glanced at him. "Were you…uh, close to your father?"

He turned his head enough for her to see the wry expression on his features. "Why do you ask? Because you think he was a mean man? Most people do."

The question took her totally by surprise and she stopped in her tracks to look at him. "I—no. I don't think your father was a mean man. He couldn't have raised four good children if that had been the case."

A dimple came and went in his cheek. "I suppose that's true. I just thought—well, it's no secret that Tucker wasn't known for his kind and gentle ways. But I guess he would have never made this ranch into what it is today by being soft." His expression turned somber as he drew in a long breath and let it out slowly. "Tucker stepped on a lot of people down through the years. I'm not going to try to deny that. But as far as being a father to us kids—he loved us. To the point of being obsessive, you could say. He wanted to guide every step we took and he wanted us flocked around him. That's why…he considered me the turncoat son. I didn't stick around to do his bidding."

The more he spoke, the more Corrina's eyebrows

lifted, until finally she was staring at him with a surprised look. "Turncoat son. That's a rather horrible way to paint yourself."

"Not really. He saw my leaving as a desertion."

"But—but you wanted to do something different with yourself. You had a right to choose the life *you* wanted to live. There's nothing wrong with that," Corrina argued.

"No. But I have to live with the knowledge that I was a disappointment to my father. That's not an easy thing to do."

His hand slipped to the curve of her waist and he nudged her forward. Corrina curbed the urge to shiver as hot and cold sensations rushed through her body and muddled her ability to focus on anything except him.

"I guess being poor made things easier for me," Corrina said, then with a mocking laugh, added, "That sounds crazy, doesn't it? Especially when my life has been anything but easy. I don't have to tell you that we didn't have much while I was growing up. And where I was concerned, my father never had any tall ambitions. Except that I get married and have kids. I honestly think it was a big relief to him when I finally married Dale and moved to Colorado. But after a while that failed." Sighing, she looked up at him. "I guess the one thing I didn't fail at is Matthew. He's a good boy, so far. Even if he is mine."

Seth smiled. "He's a fine boy, Corrina. A man couldn't do better for a son."

His compliment sent a warm rush of pleasure to the deepest part of her. "I would very much like to give him more than I have so far. That's why I'm working two jobs. I want to make sure he has the money to go to college, to make something of himself."

Seth thought about the hard work he'd seen her putting in at the Wagon Wheel. He'd also seen her father's lazy ways. No doubt she had her hands full.

"What about Matthew's father? Doesn't he pay you child support? Maybe you could put part of that aside for your son's college."

Corrina stopped again and this time she grimly shook her head. "Dale has never paid a cent of child support. I wouldn't even know where to find the man."

Seth felt an anger begin to boil deep inside him. No matter what had gone wrong between Corrina and her husband, Matthew shouldn't have to suffer because of it.

"I could find him, you know," he said. "If you wanted me to. If you wanted to make the man pay."

Something beneath her breast swelled at the idea that he was offering to help her in such a personal way. Seth had authority and connections and there was no doubt he could find Dale and put legal pressure on him.

"Thank you, Seth. But to tell you the truth, it's a relief not to have to deal with the man. And since he didn't provide for us while we were married, I seriously doubt he would now."

"There are laws against that, you know. He could go to jail."

A grimace tightened her features as she slowly shook her head. "I just want to forget him. I'm not out for vengeance. Besides, most of it's my fault for ever marrying him."

"Why did you?"

Because I couldn't have you.

The words in her heart rose up and very nearly made her groan out loud. Where had that come from? She hadn't been *that* hung up on Seth. Well, yes, she had been, she reluctantly admitted to herself. But she'd never been naive enough to pine after him, to change the course of her life because of him.

Glancing around, she spotted a boulder large enough for both of them to sit on. She walked over and eased down on the red sandstone and waited for him to join her.

Once he was sitting beside her, she said, "I married for the usual reasons, Seth. I thought I was in love with Dale."

He studied her face intently. "You thought? You didn't know if you loved him?"

A frustrated breath passed her lips. Speaking of her failed marriage was not her favorite topic. But he'd asked and she couldn't think of one good reason not to tell him.

"I was young. And I think I was bowled over with the idea of having a husband and home of my own. When Dale offered that to me I felt so…grateful. And yes, I felt love for him, too. He was good to me then, at first. But after the new wore off of our marriage he began to resent the responsibility of being married. You see, he was a dreamer, and having a wife was holding him back, or so he thought."

Beneath the brim of his black hat, a frown creased his forehead. "Why? How were you holding him back?"

She grimaced, let out a mocking laugh, then made a dismissive gesture with her hand. "I wanted him to work. To help me make a living for us."

He was silent for a moment before he let out a scornful grunt. "Oh. Sounds like you were really asking a lot from the man," he said mockingly.

She sighed. "Dale wanted to travel all over the

United States. He had an idea that he wanted to write historical fiction and, of course, he needed to travel for research. For a while he crossed several states on the money his parents would shell out to him.''

''Did you go with him?''

Corrina shook her head. ''No. I wasn't invited. Besides, someone had to stay home and pay the bills. But eventually his parents' money ran out and he was forced to stay home. That's when he shelved the book idea and decided he needed to come up with some sort of technical invention that would make him rich.'' She looked at Seth and hoped she would find understanding on his face. ''You know, I feel so stupid now. Just telling you this out loud makes me sound like an idiot for ever getting into such a situation—and for staying in it for two years. But I was young and I didn't want my marriage to fail. Especially after Matthew was born. But I finally came to the realization that Dale would never be good for Matthew or anybody. He was too self-absorbed.''

After all this time, Seth could see that she was still beating up on herself for making a mistake. No doubt she'd been telling herself that she wasn't smart enough to choose another husband or that she even deserved someone to love her.

Wanting to comfort her somehow, he reached over and took her small hand in his. Her fingers were cold, so he placed his other hand on top of hers and pressed it between his warm palms. ''Everybody has made mistakes about people, Corrina. You couldn't have known Dale would change so drastically.''

''But I should have been more careful. I shouldn't have jumped into a life with a person I'd known only a few months.''

His mouth twisted into the semblance of a smile. "Believe me, I've misjudged people before. And I'm trained in trying to read their character. But during one of the first cases I worked, there was a young man my partner suspected of being connected to a phony identification racket. I refused to believe the young man was involved. He just didn't come across as a felon to me. But later we discovered that he was and I felt like a complete fool for being duped."

"At least you didn't marry the wrong person," she said with a heavy dose of self-deprecation.

His gaze slipped from her lovely face to their clasped hands. "No. But I came close to getting married. And that would have been a big mistake," he admitted. "She wasn't willing to share me with the Rangers and thankfully I realized that before we tied the knot."

Her eyes curiously searched his face. "So you have been in love," she murmured.

Heat rushed through him, although he wasn't exactly sure if the reaction was from being so close to her or simply because they were discussing such an intimate subject.

"Well, I think I was like you," he said quietly. "My Ranger buddies were all married and had children. I thought it was time I started a family, too. Andrea was an attractive, willing woman who worked in the D.A.'s office in Bexar County. She was good at her job, but eventually I had to face up to the fact that she would never make a Ranger's wife. And when I ended our relationship, I realized I'd never really been in love. I'd just been going through the motions."

Her eyes searched his face as all sorts of questions about his life raced through her mind. "What does it take to make a Ranger's wife?"

Seth's expression turned a bit sheepish and he scuffed the toe of his boot at a rock sunk deep in the red soil. "Well, a Ranger can be called out at any time. If duty calls, birthdays, holidays and special occasions all have to be put aside. Add to that, he might be gone for days running, leaving his wife alone to care for their home and kids. Plus, there's the danger factor she has to live with every time her husband goes out the door. So she'd need to be brave and have lots of patience and understanding. Even more, she'd have to be unselfish."

"Sounds like you need a remarkable woman," she murmured.

His lips twisted ruefully. "That's why I'm not married."

In other words, he'd never met a woman who could meet up to his high standards. Well, she couldn't blame him for being so particular. If she'd been more scrupulous in choosing a husband, she might not be a single mother right now. But where did love come in with all that calculating? A person simply couldn't find the perfect person then tell him or herself to fall in love. Things just didn't work that way.

"I guess a lot has happened to us since we walked the halls of Aztec High," Corrina commented.

"Nearly twenty years has happened." He rubbed the pad of his thumb against the back of her hand and when he spoke again, his voice lowered to a husky pitch. "But I can truthfully say I never forgot you, Corrina."

Corrina swallowed as the warmth of his body and the gentle pressure of his hand around hers filled her with a longing so powerful it caused everything inside of her to tremble.

"I can't imagine that, Seth. You had plenty of friends

in high school. Especially girls. I used to hear them arguing over who was cuter, you or Ross.''

He grunted with amusement. ''Who won out? Me or Ross?''

She laughed softly as those young, carefree days came back to her. ''Usually you were considered the cutest. Mainly because you were older and more mature.''

Seth chuckled. ''Don't tell Ross that. His ego will be crushed,'' he teased and then his expression sobered. ''I'd like to ask you something, Corrina.''

Her blue eyes peeped up at him beneath her long lashes. ''About what?'' she asked guardedly.

''About you and me. Back then.''

Her heart began to pound as all sorts of thoughts darted through her head. Did he know? Had he guessed how love-struck she'd been for him? No. He couldn't know. She'd never told anyone of her feelings for Seth Ketchum. She'd been careful not to express them in any way. Especially to him.

Breathing a little easier, she moistened her lips. ''What about me and you?'' she asked carefully.

''Well, I considered you a friend. When we'd talk in the halls, you were always nice to me. But I—'' He broke off with an awkward laugh, then with a squeeze to her hand, he started again. ''I guess this is silly. Especially for me to bring it up after all the years. But I'm just curious.''

Corrina was amazed by his little display of bashfulness. It was endearing.

Casting him a brief smile, she said, ''Now you're making *me* curious.''

He grinned at her, a slow easy grin that was totally

sexy and completely disarming. "All right. I'll go on. Just promise not to laugh."

"Don't worry. It takes a lot to make me laugh," she said quietly.

As his eyes surveyed her serious face, it dawned on him that he'd never heard her laugh. Not a real, out-loud, tickled-to-death kind of laugh. When had she become so serious? he wondered. Or had she always been that way and he just hadn't known it?

"Okay. I just wanted to know whether—well, if I had asked you for a date back then, would you have turned me down?"

The question caught her so off guard that for a moment her heart stopped beating and a tight burning sensation invaded her lungs. Desperate to compose herself, she pulled her hand from his and stood. "I...uh..." She looked at him and forced herself to smile as though they were discussing the weather. "You don't mind putting a girl on the spot, do you?"

He shrugged. "I told you that you'd probably laugh."

Corrina wished she could laugh and treat his whole question as a joke. But she couldn't. Not when she could see the solemn way he was regarding her.

"I'm not laughing. I just don't know how to answer you. Or why it should even matter to you now."

He stood beside her and her knees quivered like soft gelatin. The male scent of his skin mingled with the faint scent of sandalwood and grasses. Corrina's nostrils flared as the pleasant odor stirred her senses.

"Because I've always wondered," he replied.

She cast him a sidelong glance that was unknowingly provocative. "If you'd asked me back then—" she paused and shook her head ''—I would have probably turned you down.''

Instead of looking conceitedly shocked, he nodded in grim agreement. ''That's what I thought. I always got those keep-your-distance signals from you.''

She looked down at her feet while hot color swept up her face.

''Why, Corrina?''

Her gaze darted to his face. ''You mean, why would I have turned you down?''

He nodded and she grimaced.

''This is embarrassing,'' she half whispered. ''Do we have to talk about this?''

Reaching out, Seth curled his hand around her upper arm. ''I thought we were…well, we weren't exactly what I'd call great friends, but we were friendly acquaintances back then,'' he said softly. ''I thought you liked me. But I'd somehow known that you wouldn't have dated me. That's enough to confuse any teenage boy. It still confuses me.''

Dropping her chin, she let out a long sigh. ''Oh, it wasn't that I didn't like you enough, Seth. We were so different. It would have only caused problems.''

A frown marred his forehead. ''Problems? What kind of problems?''

Lifting her head, she dared to meet his gaze. ''I was a Dawson. Do you honestly think your father would have stood by and allowed you to date a girl like me?''

He looked completely taken aback, as though that thought had never entered his head. ''What do you mean, a girl like you? You were beautiful and intelligent and a lady.''

''Yes. But I was poor. And your father—''

"My father and Rube were friends. Tucker didn't discriminate against people with less money than him."

Her chin rose a fraction. "Being friends with Daddy was one thing, but allowing his son to date Rube's daughter would have been another thing."

Seth frowned. "Did you ever stop to think I had a mind of my own? Tucker didn't choose my friends. He did manage to keep Jess away from Victoria—for a while. But thankfully she eventually came to her senses. As for Ross, he went through girls like he did boots—several a month. Dad couldn't have kept up with his choices." With a look of disbelief, he shook his head. "I never thought—you've bowled me over with this, Corrina. If I'd known what you were thinking back then—well, that's all in the past. Tucker is dead and I'm a grown man. There's no reason for you to turn me down now."

Slowly, Corrina's eyes widened. "Are you—are you asking me for a date?"

One corner of his lips curled upward and his hand loosened its grip on her arm and began to slide up and down her bare forearm. "Why not? I wanted to know you better back when we were teenagers. And I still do."

"Seth," she said with a groan and quickly turned her back to him. "I don't know what to say."

His head bent toward hers and her already weakened knees threatened to buckle. Heat tingled along her arm where his fingers slid seductively against her skin.

"I can tell you what I want you to say," he murmured. "Say that you're glad I'll be here for the next three weeks. And that you'd like to get to know me better, too."

She was drunk, Corrina thought wildly. Besotted by

the touch of his hand and the husky growl of his voice. She had to mentally slap herself and wake up from the spell he was weaving over her.

"I—it would be foolish to start something when…you're going to be leaving soon." Another thought struck her and she slowly turned to face him. "Seth, you didn't take Matthew riding today—you weren't using him to get to me, were you?"

The question sounded ridiculous, even to her own ears. He could have most any woman he wanted. He didn't need to play games with a divorcée. Still, she couldn't stop the doubts of his motives from swirling through her mind.

Frowning, he stepped closer and in a soft but edgy voice, he said, "I'd like to pretend I never heard that question."

He was clearly insulted, perhaps even hurt by her suggestion, but Corrina couldn't help it. After all she'd been through with Dale, she was suspicious of every man's intentions.

"I'm sorry if—if I'm being rude," she stammered, her heart beating a mile a minute. "But—but I just can't believe…that you could be interested in me—or Matthew."

"Why?"

She made a helpless gesture with her hand as her head slowly swung back and forth. "Because you're Seth Ketchum. You're rich and you're a Texas Ranger. Do I need to keep going?"

He closed his hands around her shoulders and she quivered with intense longing as his hazel eyes delved into hers.

"I can't believe you think so little of yourself. And your son."

"I don't—"

"Your son is a wonderful boy. And you are an extremely attractive woman. Being a Ketchum, a Ranger or having money doesn't make me blind or a snob," he said gruffly.

Groaning with frustration, she closed her eyes and wondered how their conversation had ever gotten to this point. "I didn't say you were a snob," she whispered desperately.

His hand came up to cup her cheek and the warm, intimate contact caused her eyes to pop wide open.

"Corrina, you're trembling like a leaf. Why are you afraid of me? I would never hurt you."

Oh yes you would. You'd show me a glimpse of heaven, then take it all away when you head back to Texas.

"I—I'm not afraid. I…just don't understand what you want from me."

His lips twisted. "I don't know that myself, Corrina. I just know that I've wanted to do this from the moment I saw you standing on your daddy's porch."

Her lips parted to question him. But he didn't give her the chance. His head bent downward and then his lips were softly touching hers.

Shock momentarily froze her and she stood motionless as he pressed a kiss at each corner of her mouth, in the middle of her chin, and the tip of her nose. By the time he returned to her lips, heat was suffusing her body, waking every latent desire inside of her with a reckless vengeance.

Before she realized what she was doing, she was on her tiptoes, straining to return his kiss. A tiny moan sounded deep in her throat as her arms crept around his neck, her body arched into his.

Seth had only meant to kiss her once. He'd only intended to make soft contact with her lips, to taste her, to let her know in a small way that he wanted her. That was all he'd planned. He'd not counted on her tasting like strong, sweet wine. Nor had he expected the sudden jolt he'd felt to the bottom of his feet. Now he couldn't stop. He didn't want to stop.

Corrina was thinking she'd never been kissed before. Not like this. Not where the whole world around her was spinning, the ground beneath her feet tilting.

Just as she was telling herself she had to pull away from him, a high, mournful sound echoed across the darkening mesa. The savage noise was enough to break the spell of the kiss and allow her the strength to tear her mouth from his.

With goose bumps racing across her skin, she shivered and stared out at the gathering darkness. "Was that a coyote?" she whispered hoarsely.

The moment Seth started to answer, the coyote's soulful howl reverberated around them. Corrina unwittingly edged closer to the security of Seth's solid body.

"Yes. Don't be scared," he said in a hushed voice. "He's only calling to his mate."

Her eyes darted up to his face. "You don't know that," she scoffed. "He's probably howling with hunger."

He laid a finger upon his lips. "Listen and you'll hear for yourself."

Her heart pounding from the aftermath of his kisses and the darkening wilderness surrounding them, Corrina stood stock-still and waited for an answering howl.

It came in a matter of seconds, far across the opposite side of the mesa. The sound was so lonesome and pleading that tears filled Corrina's eyes. Quickly she wiped at them with the back of her hand and turned her head so that he wouldn't guess she'd become emotional.

"See," he said, his hand settling on her shoulder. "I told you. Once a coyote mates, it's for life. They work together to raise and feed their family. And they never get too far from each other."

Corrina closed her eyes as his fingers began to gently knead her flesh. She'd never wanted any man like she'd wanted Seth a few minutes ago and now she felt as if she'd never be the same.

Clearing her throat, she said, "I've heard if one of them dies or gets killed, he or she chooses another mate and starts over. Sort of like a second chance, I guess," she added on a wistful note.

"Yeah. Everybody deserves a second chance at happiness, Corrina. Even you."

Her heart heavy, she turned back to him. "We'd better go. It's getting dark and Matthew will be looking for us."

She started to walk away, but the grip he had on her shoulder prevented her from taking a step.

"What about seeing me again?" he asked softly.

"I'll...I'll have to think about it," she told him. And before he could push the subject further, she twisted out of his grasp and hurried back down the trail.

Chapter Six

More than an hour later, Corrina was still shaken from Seth's heated kisses. As he drove her and Matthew home, she did her best to make casual conversation, but once they arrived at her father's place, she tossed him a quick goodbye and hurried into the house before anything else could be said between them.

She was in the kitchen going through the motions of tidying the counters when she heard her son enter the house through the front door.

"Matthew, you'd better head for the shower and get ready for bed," she called to him.

His boots scuffed across the linoleum as he walked into the kitchen. "Aw, Mom, it's still early. I want to watch TV with Pa."

"You've had a long day, Matt. It'll be your bedtime by the time you finish your shower."

He grimaced and opened his mouth to protest, but he

quickly seemed to have second thoughts, and instead of arguing he shrugged his shoulders in acquiescence.

"Okay, Mom."

Corrina sighed with relief as she watched him leave the room. Thank goodness Matthew hadn't put up a big fight. She wasn't in the mood to deal with that sort of thing tonight. Her mind was whirling, her nerves standing straight on end.

For the past hour she'd been telling herself to relax, to forget about kissing Seth Ketchum, but she might as well have been talking to the dog. Cotton would have paid way more attention to her advice than she had.

Realizing her hands were gripped together, she purposely forced them to her sides and walked over to the coffeemaker. Caffeine couldn't send her nerves flying any higher than they already were, she thought, and maybe the act of doing something mundane would help calm her.

"Corrina? Are you in there, honey?"

The sound of her father's voice suddenly interrupted her plans for coffee and she walked out to the small living room where he was sitting in an armchair in front of the television. A boxing match that had taken place more than thirty years ago was playing on the Classic Sports Channel.

Rube liked to live in the past any way he could. Probably because he didn't have much of a future, she thought sadly.

"Yes, Dad? Did you want something?"

He looked at her and for one brief moment she thought she glimpsed a shadow of worry in his eyes. But that was a silly notion. Rube never worried about anything. And since he never had, it would certainly be late for him to take up the habit now.

She realized she was right as a ragged grin twisted his lips. "No. I just thought you might sit down with your old dad and tell him about your evening."

"I—I really have several things to do before I go to bed. Remember, I'm working tomorrow."

Disappointment swept over his face and Corrina immediately felt guilty. He wasn't asking for much and she should be glad her father was interested in her life. One day he'd be gone and then she'd be like Seth— missing his father and wishing he could somehow bring back the moments with him.

"Well, there's really not that much to tell," she said as she eased down on the end of the couch. "Except that I had a good time."

Rube aimed the remote control at the television set and lowered the volume before he looked her way. Corrina was surprised. Normally when he was watching sports, no one got his attention.

"That's real good. Real good." He thoughtfully rubbed his whiskered chin. "I guess the T Bar K was just as pretty as ever."

His statement puzzled her and she wondered vaguely if her father was beginning to suffer the early stages of dementia. Lord only knew he'd drunk enough alcohol in his time to ruin a big part of his brain cells.

"I wouldn't know, Dad. Until tonight, I'd never been there before."

He looked at her and frowned. "Yeah. I guess you're right. Guess I never did take you over there with me when I used to visit Tucker. My mistake, honey. If I had, you might have been married to Seth a long time ago."

"Dad!" she gasped. "I don't want to hear that kind of talk."

He twisted around in his chair so he could look at her squarely. "What's the matter? I'm just speakin' the truth. You always were a mighty pretty girl, Corrina."

Corrina wasn't about to point out the social differences between the Dawsons and the Ketchums. Sighing with frustration, she said, "Dad, you make it sound like a young girl goes out and purposely snags herself a husband."

"Well, sure they do. You'd be a fool to think they don't. Women ain't no different than men, honey. The smart ones take advantage of a good opportunity."

A good opportunity being money, Corrina thought. How ironic and sad that her father was so taken with the idea of money, when he'd never made much of an effort to acquire any for himself or his own family.

"I understand there are some women like that," Corrina said flatly. "But not me. That's not what marriage should be about."

Rube snorted. "You married for love, Corrina. And look what it got you. Dale couldn't take care of himself, much less you or Matthew. He was worthless."

And what did you do all those years you were married to my mother? she asked silently, then immediately shamed herself for even questioning her father's past behavior. He had always provided a home for them, such as it was. And he'd always been around to love them. In Corrina's opinion that counted far more than money.

"I don't know why you're talking this way, Dad," she said, puzzled. "Seth doesn't have those sorts of ideas about me."

Her father's eyebrows lifted. "Why not? You'd like him to, wouldn't you?"

Her mouth very nearly gaped open, but she managed

to press her lips together to stop the look of shock she was feeling at her father's question. Had she been going around the past few days with stars in her eyes? Had her father somehow guessed how she felt about Seth Ketchum? No. He couldn't. *She* didn't even understand her feelings for the Texas Ranger.

Forcing a light laugh, she said, "Dad, that's a foolish question to be asking me. Seth is only here for a few weeks."

Rube studied his daughter's guarded face. "How many weeks?"

Uneasy by the sudden interest her father was showing in her private life, she frowned and evaded the truth. "I don't know exactly. That's not really any of my business."

He shrugged as though his question hadn't really been all that important anyway. "Well, you could make it your business if you were of a mind to."

She didn't know where he was getting these strange ideas or suggestions. Since she'd come home to live, he'd not encouraged her once to find a husband.

Rising from her seat, she walked over to her father and laid a hand upon his shoulder. "What's the matter, Dad? Are you worried that I might find someone and move away from here?"

Gruffly, he cleared his throat. "No."

She sighed. "Well, you needn't be worrying about that. I'm not in any hurry to put myself, or Matthew, into another man's hands. Besides, who would take care of you?"

Rube looked up and Corrina's heart went heavy at the sad resignation in his eyes. "You can't take care of me forever, girl. And if you was to get hooked up with Seth, I'd at least die knowing you were taken care of."

His somber talk piled onto her already raw nerves. This conversation wasn't what she needed at the moment. But she tried to humor him with a wry smile and a pat on the shoulder before she moved away from his chair.

At the doorway, she glanced back at him, and worry for his health flickered through her. For some reason tonight, his shoulders appeared more slumped, his graying hair thinner and the lines on his ruddy face etched deeper.

"I don't need a man to take care of me, Dad. Matthew and I are doing fine right here with you."

His reaction was a look of disapproval before he turned up the volume and focused his attention back on the television screen.

With another weary sigh, Corrina hurried down the short hallway to the bathroom. Except for a scattering of towels and a wet floor, the room was empty.

Promising herself to come back and tidy it later, Corrina walked to her son's bedroom and found him dressed in pajama bottoms and lying atop the covers of his small oak bed. Tossed over the footboard were the scarred leather chaps Seth had given him. Next to the head of the bed, in a rope-bottom chair, lay the spurs. Corrina knew the gifts meant more to the boy than anything he'd ever received.

"All ready for bed?" she asked.

His head bobbed up and down against the pillow. "I'm kinda gettin' tired now."

Corrina smiled wanly. "It's about time. You've had a big day."

He grinned sleepily. "Yeah. It was great, wasn't it?"

Without waiting for her to reply, he turned his blue eyes toward the ceiling. "That ranch—the T Bar K—

is really somethin'. I didn't know people around here lived like that.''

Guilt that she'd not been able to provide more for Matthew than what she had, hit her hard. But just as quickly she told herself that sort of thinking was foolish. Not everyone could be rich. Not everyone needed to be rich. And what she'd done for herself and her boy had been through decent, hard work. She should be proud of that.

Slowly, Corrina sank onto the edge of Matthew's bed. ''The Ketchums are the only ones around here who live like that, Matt. But that doesn't necessarily mean they're any happier than we are.''

Matthew shrugged one shoulder. ''Guess not.'' He looked at his mother and grinned. ''Seth don't seem to care about money, though. That's the way Aaron is, too. They don't act like they're better than me.''

''That's because they're not. They're just regular folks like you and me.''

Who was she trying to fool? she wondered dryly. Seth wasn't just a regular guy. There wasn't anything *regular* about him.

Her troubled thoughts continued to whirl as she watched Matthew reach over and pick up one of the spurs. With the tip of his forefinger, he lovingly traced the silver pattern etched into the band.

''You know what these kind of spurs are called, Mom? I do, 'cause Seth told me. He said cowboys have been wearing these kind since way back—when there was outlaws and posses.''

Even though she had no idea as to its kind, Corrina made a big deal of inspecting the spur. ''Hmm. I don't know much about a cowboy's tack. Guess you'll have to tell me, son.''

With proud importance, he rose on one elbow and peeked up at her through the blond hair that had flopped onto his forehead. "It's a jinglebob spur. See?" He used the tip of his finger to flip a little bell attached to the rowel. "They make a jinglin' noise when you walk. That's so people can hear you comin'."

Smiling gently, she reached up and pushed the hair off his forehead. "You like the things Seth gave you, don't you?"

"I sure do!" He flopped onto his back and rested the spur in the middle of his chest. "I like Seth, too. A whole lot. Don't you?"

Emotion poured into her heart and filled it so full that a bittersweet pain wound its way between her breasts.

Rising from the bed, she answered softly, "Yes. He's a very nice man. Now it's time for you to go to sleep. Get under the sheet and I'll turn out the light."

At the door, she waited for him to get settled before she flipped off the light switch. "Good night, sweetie."

"Mom?"

"Yes."

"I—well, I just wonder why Seth don't have a boy or a girl of his own."

Corrina was glad she was standing in the dark. She wouldn't have wanted Matthew to see how much his question had knocked her off guard.

"Well, Seth isn't married, Matthew. He's never had a wife to give him a child."

"Oh." There was a long pause and then he added, "I wonder why he never got a wife?"

Seth's words from earlier this evening were suddenly waltzing through Corrina's head.

She'd need to be brave, have lots of patience and understanding. Even more, she'd have to be unselfish.

In other words, Corrina thought, Seth wanted and needed a special woman. Something she would never be.

To Matthew she said, "Well, that's his private business, Matt. But I suspect he has plenty of reasons for not having a wife. Being a Ranger keeps him pretty busy."

"Yeah, I guess you're right," Matthew mumbled. "But he must be awfully lonely."

Lonely? No, Corrina doubted that Seth had ever really been lonely. Not like she'd been these years since her divorce. Seth had siblings and an exciting job that kept him too busy to think about living without the love of a wife.

Yet she'd felt a searching hunger in his kiss and she'd responded to it with all her heart. If that made her a fool, she couldn't help it. All she could do now was make sure she didn't get that close to him again.

The next morning, shortly after breakfast, Seth received a call from Jess. The undersheriff had some things to show Seth that he might find interesting. Could he drive into the Aztec?

Seth didn't question his brother-in-law as to what sort of things. Instead, he quickly ended the call and told Marina he'd be gone from the ranch for a few hours.

Thirty minutes later, he pulled into a parking slot in front of a redbrick building that served as the headquarters for the entire sheriff's department. Since Seth had moved to Texas, two wings had been added to the structure and when he stepped inside, he could see the interior had been newly remodeled, also. His old hometown was making progress with the times, he thought, as he approached a desk where a young female officer was busily typing at an up-to-date computer.

Glancing away from her work, she peered up at him. "Yes?"

"I'm here to see Undersheriff Hastings," he said.

The perceptible arch of her brows said he was the most interesting thing she'd seen in days. Or maybe she eyeballed every man who walked through the door, Seth thought.

"Your name?"

"Seth Ketchum."

Her lips formed a silent "o" and she immediately rose from her seat and began to stutter. "Oh...uh... yes...you..."

"Calm down, Rebecca, Seth isn't going to eat you."

Seth instantly recognized Jess's voice and he turned to his left to see his brother-in-law's tall, lanky frame sauntering toward him.

Stepping away from the desk and the red-faced young officer, Seth greeted the other man with a handshake. "Good to see you this morning, Jess."

"Same here." He gestured toward the hallway behind him. "Let's go to my office," he invited.

Nodding, Seth moved into step beside the other lawman.

"What was wrong with that officer back there?" Seth asked. "Does she have a peculiar speaking problem?"

Jess chuckled lowly. "No. She's normally smooth and efficient. The sight of you shook her."

A comical frown creased Seth's face. "Me? I don't get it."

Jess cast him a wry look as he ushered Seth through an open door to the right. "Everyone in this building knows who you are and what you are. I'll give them fifteen minutes and they'll be knocking on the door to meet you.''

Shaking his head, Seth sank into a wooden chair angled in front of Jess's desk. ''I'm sure you've had FBI agents and other high ranking law officials here in Aztec before. I'm not anything special.''

''No, you're just a Texas Ranger,'' he said with mocking amusement. ''That's no big deal to a little county deputy. Or do you remember what it's like to be a county deputy?''

Seth chuckled. ''Yeah. It's been a long time ago. But I guess I do remember. I'll go say hello to your staff once we finish talking,'' he promised.

''Thanks, Seth. It'll be a morale booster.'' The undersheriff walked over to one corner of the room and picked up a cardboard box. After he'd carried it to his desk, he carefully opened the top and motioned for Seth to have a look inside.

''What is it?'' Seth asked as he rose from the chair.

''Evidence. What little there is.''

Seth tossed a questioning look at him. ''The Noah Rider case?''

Jess nodded. ''Sheriff Perez agreed that I should show it to you.''

''Have you gone through it yet?'' Seth asked him.

Jess gave him another grim nod. ''Yeah. There's not a whole lot there. But hopefully you can pick up something from it that we might have missed.''

''I don't know about that,'' Seth said doubtfully. He reached down and picked up a folder marked autopsy report. ''Tell me about this.''

''Not a whole lot to tell. Small caliber hole in the back of the skull. Noah probably never knew what hit him. Also, the coroner believes the body had lain out in the elements for at least two weeks before it was discovered.''

''Any hairs or unusual fibers found on his clothing?''

''I don't know about unusual. But a number of horse hairs were identified from his jacket and jeans. Gray and black in color.''

Seth unconsciously rubbed a thumb against his chin. ''Hmm. From the same horse?''

''No. Two different horses. Which supports the theory that Noah had ridden onto T Bar K land with his killer.''

Seth nodded soberly. ''Sounds like it, doesn't it?'' He glanced down at the contents of the box. ''Anything else interesting in here?''

''Not much. Except for Noah's bank records.''

''What about them?''

''The man made a substantial withdrawal every month. The same amount, the same time.''

''I take it this withdrawal wasn't a check written to another person?''

With a huge sigh, Jess walked around the desk and took a seat. Seth followed his example and settled himself in the wooden chair opposite his brother-in-law.

''Apparently Noah wrote a check to himself every month with the word *cash* written in the memo line. Who got the cash is beyond me.''

Jess picked up a pen and absently tapped it against the ink blotter on the desk. ''How do you go about tracking something like that down, Seth? Or is the money even important to this case?''

Resting his elbows on his knees, Seth leaned forward. ''It could be very important. Or it could be the man just liked to do his business with cash. Was there any mail in Noah's house that might lead us somewhere?''

Jess grimaced. "That's another thing. Deputy Red-wing couldn't find any personal mail. There were the usual utility bills and junk mail, but other than that, nothing. Not even a Christmas card from a friend or relative."

Sadness fell upon Seth's shoulders as he stared pensively at the dusty window behind Jess's shoulder. "Noah must have lived a lonely life."

"Yeah. That's what Victoria said. It's cut her up to think he died believing no one cared about him."

Jess nodded. "I know what she means. I feel guilty because I never made the effort to keep in touch with him. Especially after all he'd done for the Ketchum family. But people move on and so does life."

Just the way it had for Corrina and him, Seth thought. Their lives had taken different directions. Time had clicked by, yet their paths had crossed again. Was that coincidence or fate, he wondered. And whose path had Noah Rider crossed?

Rising to his feet, Seth looked into the box that was filled with reports and physical evidence zipped carefully in plastic bags. "I'd like to take a few minutes to look through all this," he said to Jess.

The undersheriff nodded. "Take all the time you need. I have some things to do, so you can have my office to yourself. If you need anything, just ask for it. I'll see you later."

"Thanks, Jess."

More than two hours later, Seth walked out of the Sheriff's department building. After immersing himself in the dark and somber evidence of Noah's murder, the bright morning sun was a welcome sight. Before he climbed into his truck, he lifted his face to the sky and let the warmth and the light push away the heavy mind-set and make way for more pleasant thoughts.

Almost instantly, the image of Corrina entered his mind and the sudden urge for a cup of coffee had him quickly climbing into his truck and making a left at the next intersection where the street would take him right by the Wagon Wheel.

"Coffee, hell," he muttered with a snort. Who was he kidding? He'd drink coal oil if it would give him a chance to see Corrina again.

Since last night and their walk on the mesa, Seth had felt like a moonstruck teenager. A condition he'd never experienced before. And one he certainly didn't understand.

He honestly didn't know what had come over him. It wasn't like him to go after a woman. He hardly ever *thought* about women. He didn't have time. And frankly, he'd decided a long time ago that he and women didn't mix. Maybe he expected too much. Or maybe he was already married to his job. Either way, it didn't matter. He'd steered clear of the opposite sex, and as far as he was concerned, he'd been happier for it.

But something had happened to him the moment he'd seen Corrina again. And last night—God help him— just the thought of how she'd felt in his arms was working chaos with his head. A part of him was shocked that he'd touched her, talked to her so intimately. He hadn't planned what had happened between them. And even if he had, he wouldn't have anticipated Corrina's passionate reaction. Now he couldn't get it, or her, out of his thoughts.

After parking his truck in the nearest space he could

find, he entered the Wagon Wheel and was mildly surprised to see the café nearly empty of customers.

Sliding into the first booth he came to, Seth glanced around for a waitress—*the* waitress, he mentally corrected himself. But rather than spotting Corrina's graceful figure behind the bar, an older woman with a thick waist and carrot-blond hair was wiping down a glass pie case.

She took her time coming to the booth, but Seth didn't care. He purposely lived on Texas time. It was better for his heart and his peace of mind.

"Good morning," she greeted. "What'cha need? Cook has closed down the breakfast grill, but we have some pastries left. Or pie. Or you could go ahead and order lunch, but the special won't be ready for another hour or so." She tapped a forefinger thoughtfully against her chin. "Still, you could get something from the menu. Any of that interest you?"

He glanced at the woman's name tag as he gave her a slow smile. "Sounds like I came in at a bad time, Betty."

She waved a hand in a dismissive gesture and then quickly narrowed her eyes at him. "I don't mean to be nosy, mister, but do you happen to be from Texas?"

"I am," he said, expecting to hear she had family in Dallas or Houston or Waco, that the weather was too hot and sticky there, and the people too damn proud for her taste. Instead, she hurried away from the booth as though someone had shouted there was a fire in the kitchen.

"Just wait right there," she called over her shoulder. "Don't move."

Betty disappeared behind a pair of swinging doors and Seth was trying to figure out what the waitress was up to, when he noticed Corrina emerging from the same swinging doors. She glanced furtively at the coffee drinkers in the back of the room and then hurried toward his booth.

The pleasure he felt at seeing her again curved the corners of his lips. "Good morning," he greeted as she came to a stop at the edge of the table.

"Good morning," she replied.

Her cheeks were tinged with pink and her bosom was heaving slightly, as though she'd been arguing or was agitated about something. Maybe it was his being here that had her stirred up, he thought. Lord only knew how much she agitated him.

"I—uh—had to come into the sheriff's office," he explained. "I thought I'd drop by and have a cup of coffee."

She let out a long breath. "Betty should have gotten it for you. I'm sorry about that."

His eyelids lowered subtly as his gaze wandered over the fresh beauty of her face. Her pale skin and soft full lips begged to be kissed and he was just the man to do it, he realized. The male arrogance of his thoughts took him by surprise, but then a lot of things had surprised him since he'd seen Corrina again.

"I'm not a bit sorry," he drawled. "I wanted to see you more than drink coffee."

If the diner hadn't been so quiet, he probably wouldn't have heard the sharp little intake of her breath. As it was, the sound was strangely erotic to his ears.

"Seth—"

"Maybe you'd better go get the coffee," he interrupted.

With a worried frown, she left the booth and he watched her go behind the counter and fill a cup from a glass carafe. As she carried it and a saucer back to the table, he couldn't keep his eyes off the gentle sway of her body or the long, smooth length of her legs exposed by the short hem of her denim skirt.

"You didn't get yourself any," he said when she placed the drink in front of him.

"I can't. I'm on duty."

He glanced pointedly around the room. "There's nothing going on in here. Surely you can use a break and I'm betting that Betty will cover for you."

The other woman would be only too glad, Corrina thought with embarrassment. "Betty needs to mind her own business," Corrina muttered.

With an amused chuckle, Seth reminded himself to make a point to thank the other waitress for sending Corrina out to him.

"Don't be sour. It's a beautiful morning. Get yourself a cup of coffee. And a piece of pie," he added. "I might want a bite of it."

Share a piece of pie with Seth Ketchum? It was the last thing she needed to be doing. In fact, if she had a lick of sense at all, she'd finish her business of waiting on him and run straight back to the sanctuary of the kitchen.

But running wasn't really what she wanted to do, she decided. Not when the very sight of his rugged face was filling her heart with a joy she hadn't felt in years.

A tentative smile came and went on her lips. "All right," she agreed softly. "I'll be right back."

Moments later, she returned to the table and pushed a piece of two-crust cherry pie toward him.

A corner of Seth's lips twisted upward. "How did you know I liked cherry?"

She breathed deeply and told herself to relax. She

was here in the Wagon Wheel. Seth couldn't kiss her in this public place. And she couldn't make a fool of herself by kissing him back.

Her gaze drifted to the tabletop and remained there as she tried to forget the unabashed way she'd responded to him last night. There was no telling what he'd been thinking of her. Probably that she was a fast-and-loose divorcée. Well, as bad as that was, it was better than the truth, she decided. He wouldn't understand that she'd been secretly carrying a torch for him for nearly twenty years. How could he, when she didn't understand it herself?

"An educated guess. Most men like cherry."

From the corner of her eye, she could see him pick up his cup. There was a long pause while he took a careful sip of the hot brew.

"How was Matthew this morning?" he asked.

"I left the house before daylight. He was still asleep."

"I hope I didn't wear him out too much yesterday. We rode for several miles."

She lifted her head and met his gaze. "Not at all. He was still wired up when he went to bed." And so was his mother, she thought dismally. It had been the wee hours of the morning before she'd finally been able to settle her senses and fall asleep. And later, when the alarm clock had woken her, she'd not known whether to laugh or cry about the night before.

"I sure did enjoy your son's company yesterday, Corrina."

The compliment warmed her like a candle flame glowing in a soft, dark night. It was nice to hear she was a good mother from her co-workers, but hearing it from Seth made each word special.

''Thank you, Seth. It's nice to know my son behaves himself even when I'm not around. 'Course, I don't know if that will change once he reaches his teens.''

He slipped another bite of pie into his mouth as his gaze searched her face. ''Maybe you'll be married by then and Matthew will have a stepfather to help guide him.''

Seth's softly spoken suggestion very nearly rocked her backward. ''I...'' She paused, a tiny frown marring her forehead as she stared into her coffee cup. ''I very much doubt that, Seth.''

His eyebrows arched. ''Why?''

A heavy weight suddenly settled in the middle of Corrina's chest. She'd had her chance at marriage and it hadn't worked. Maybe Seth believed in second chances, but she wasn't at all sure that she did.

''Well,'' she began, ''it's not every day that a person meets someone they...want to spend the rest of their life with. That's a rare thing.''

He pushed the pie toward her and handed her the fork. ''Yeah, you're right about that. But if a person's looking, she'd have more of a chance of finding that someone.''

Her glance went from him to the fork and back again. ''Why are you giving me your fork?''

''For the pie,'' he explained, then gestured for her to take a bite. ''I don't have too many germs.''

Did he honestly think she was worried about germs after the kisses they'd shared last night? If she could relax, even for a second, she would have found that idea very funny. But she couldn't relax. Her heart was drumming in her chest and her body was remembering all too well what it had been like to be in this man's arms.

Slowly, she sliced into the pie, took a bite and forced

herself to chew and swallow. "Believe me, Seth. I'm not looking. Not after…the ordeal I went through with Dale."

He grimaced. "Surely you don't think all men are like him."

She shook her head. "No. But how would I know? I didn't have a clue that Dale was hiding his true colors." She sliced into the pie again, not out of hunger but as a way to release nervous energy. "And anyway," she added, "I'm happy just as I am."

"Are you?"

The question made the weight in her chest just that much heavier, yet she did her best to smile at him, albeit weakly. "Of course I am. I have my son and father. Nice friends that I work with here and at school, a roof over my head and all the necessities. I don't need more than that."

If that were the case, then her wants were small, Seth thought. "Then I guess it isn't all that important for you to find Matthew a father."

She placed the fork on the empty dessert plate. "No. No, that's far down on my list of needs."

"Is that fair to him?"

Anger flared up in her. How dare he think she would put herself before her son. Her eyes darted up to meet his. "I don't know about being fair, but it's much better than giving him a stepfather who…turned out bad."

Before he could say more, she rose to her feet and began to stack the dirty dishes. "I've got to get back to work, Seth. I've already sat here too long."

He reached over and covered her hand with his. "I'm sorry if I offended you, Corrina. That wasn't my intention. In fact, I didn't really come in here to talk to you about any of that—one thing just led to another."

She was spineless, she thought miserably. All he had to do was touch her and she lost all resistance. The mild anger that had rushed through her a moment ago now drained away like muddy water, and in its place came warm sunshine.

Her eyes settled back on his face. "What *did* you come here for?" she asked bluntly.

He didn't hesitate. "To see you. To ask you about having dinner with me tonight. Just the two of us."

Her heart leaped with unexpected pleasure, yet she was careful to hide it in her words. "I had dinner with you last night."

"What does that hurt?"

"I shouldn't be out two nights in a row."

He chuckled. "I thought you were a grown woman."

She frowned at him. "I am. But I hate to leave Dad alone again."

"Surely your father and Matthew can do without you for a few hours."

They could, Corrina thought. But other than just giving him a flat-out no, her son and father were the only excuses she could think of to turn him down. After a moment's hesitation, she decided to be truthful with him. "Seth—last night—I don't think it would be wise for me to go out with you."

His hand tightened on hers. "Don't be scared, Corrina," he said gently. "Last night was nice. Very nice. And you know it."

Yes, she did know it and everything inside of her wanted to experience it all again, to be with this man that had lingered in her thoughts for nearly two decades.

"I'm a practical woman, Seth."

A grin spread his lips and exposed his very white

teeth. Just looking at him made her breath catch in her throat.

"Even practical women have to eat. I'll pick you up about six."

"I can see why you became a Texas Ranger," she commented wryly. "You like to live dangerously."

He chuckled softly and the curve on his lips was wicked enough to curl her toes. "Tonight won't be dangerous. It'll be enjoyable. I promise."

Enjoyable? Yes, spending time with Seth was more than that, she thought. It made her happier than she could ever remember being. And that was the problem. She couldn't allow herself to fall in love with a man who would be leaving in a few weeks.

"Seth, I..."

The bell above the diner door jingled, causing the remainder of her words to trail away. Glancing around, Corrina recognized the Garrisons, an older couple who were regular lunch customers at the Wagon Wheel. The husband and wife always insisted that she be their waitress, and since they never failed to reward her with a hefty tip, she could hardly dawdle here by Seth's table and argue with him about dinner tonight.

Mrs. Garrison waved at her and Corrina waved back. Quickly, she glanced back down to Seth. "All right," she said in a hushed rush. "I'll be ready at six. Now I've got to get to work."

"Good. I'll be there," he said and smiled as she hurried away.

Chapter Seven

"Are you going back to the T Bar K?"

From her seat in front of the tiny dressing table, Corrina glanced over at her son who was standing in the open doorway of her bedroom. She'd expected him to be upset that he'd not been invited to join them, yet he seemed anything but troubled. The moment she'd announced she was going out to dinner with Seth tonight, he'd been strangely jubilant.

"I don't know, Matthew. Seth didn't say where we'd be going."

He grinned. "Well, it doesn't matter. You'll have fun."

Smiling faintly, she fastened a rhinestone clip to one side of her curly hair. "You think so, huh?"

"Sure! You won't have to cook. And Seth is nice. Real nice!"

Nice, just not marriage material. If she could keep

that in the forefront of her mind while Seth was here, then she might survive his stay without getting her heart broken into a thousand pieces.

Rising to her feet, she smoothed the front of her wrapped skirt and straightened the V-necked knit top she'd chosen to wear with it. The top was a deep coral color that complemented her fiery hair and matched the summery print of her skirt. The outfit was definitely casual, but casual was the only sort of clothes she owned.

"I brought you and Pa some food from the diner for supper. It's chicken-fried steak. All you have to do is put it in the microwave and heat it. I've already told Pa, so he'll know what to do."

"Don't worry about us," Matthew assured her in his most grown-up voice. "We'll be fine."

Corrina dabbed perfume behind her ears. "You sound pretty sure about that."

"I am."

She looked at him with amused curiosity. "You act as though you're glad I'm going out to dinner with Seth. Aren't you just a little bit peeved that you're not going, too?"

He wrinkled his nose at her. "Shoot, no! I've been wantin' you to get a boyfriend for a long time and now you've got one. And he's a real Texas Ranger!"

Corrina groaned inwardly at her son's reasoning. "Oh, Matt. Don't you understand that Seth is only going to be here for a short time?" She walked over and put her hand gently on his shoulder. "I'm glad that you like Seth so much. But he won't be around forever."

Grimacing, Matthew scuffed the toe of his boot against the worn carpet. "Well, nobody is around forever, Mom. People die and leave."

Matthew's morbid remark took Corrina by complete surprise. For a moment she didn't know how to respond to her son, who seemed to think that death would be the only thing that might separate him and Seth. Dear God, what was she going to do? Matthew had already been deserted by his father. It was a hard fact the child had to live with every day. Once Seth left to go back to Texas, her son was going to think he'd been deserted a second time.

"Well, this is more than just about dying, Matt. Seth has a job in Texas, remember?"

"Yeah. But he—"

His words halted as Rube suddenly walked up and slung his arm around his grandson's shoulders. "What're you doing in here, boy? I thought me and you were gonna go burn that pile of old lumber out by the barn."

Matthew looked at his grandfather with eager surprise. "You mean it?"

Rube patted his shoulder. "Sure I do. You go get on your old boots and I'll find some kerosene and matches. We're gonna get this place around here cleaned up. We might even decide to build a new barn and get another horse to go with Blackjack."

Corrina stared at her father. What had suddenly gotten into him? she wondered. He didn't have the money to build a barn or buy a horse. And he hadn't lifted a finger to clean up around the place in at least a year. Now that she was going on a date with Seth, he suddenly decides he wants to stack old lumber and burn it. The abrupt switch in his attitude more than amazed her.

"What about your arthritis, Dad?"

He waved a dismissive hand at her. "I feel as limber as a goose today. Must be the heat."

And the empty six-pack carton she'd found in the trash, she thought dismally. Aloud, she said, "Well, that's good. But I really wish you'd put the chore off to a time when I'm here. If the fire gets out of control, this whole place could go up in flames."

He swatted another hand at her. "Hell, you act like your ol' dad doesn't have sense enough to do what I've done all my life around this ranch. There's not a bit of wind, honey, and I'll take the water hose with us. Don't be a worrywart."

"Yeah, Mom. Don't be a worrywart," Matthew backed up his grandfather.

"Me and Matthew want to roast marshmallows for dessert tonight anyway," Rube added. "You just go on and have a good time with your Texas Ranger."

Knowing she couldn't argue with the two of them, she let out a long breath and picked up a lacy shawl from the foot of her bed. "All right, Dad, I trust you to take care of things."

Matthew scurried down the hall to change his boots and Rube shook his head with reproof.

"It's a good thing you're going out tonight," he said. "You're beginning to act like an old mother hen."

Corrina whirled around to dispute his words, but the doorway was empty and she heard her father's footsteps moving on down the hallway.

Slowly, she walked over and stood before the mirror on the dressing table. Mother hen? She stared at her image. She was thirty-five. That wasn't old. She was basically still a young woman.

But you're beginning to act old.

The voice in her head was too strong to ignore, and for a few more moments she studied her reflection as though she was seeing a different woman.

For the past ten years following her divorce she'd focused her whole life on providing for her son and raising him the best way she knew how. Until her father had called her for help two years ago, nothing else had deviated her plans. And after moving back to the Dawson ranch, she'd been even more tied to her role of caretaker. It was no wonder she acted as a mother hen, she thought glumly.

Leaning closer to her reflection, she touched a finger to her cheek. Did Seth see her in the same way? Did he see her as a person who took life so seriously that she rarely smiled or laughed? Or even worse, that she was too afraid to let herself be a woman?

The fact that she was even asking herself such questions implied that she was headed for trouble. But she decided to put that worrisome thought out of her head. Once Seth went back to Texas she'd have plenty of time to be a mother hen. Right now she wanted to be a woman.

Less than five minutes later, Seth arrived, and as he helped her into his truck, he glanced toward the house and down at the barn.

"Where's Matthew?" he asked. "I was going to say hello."

"Oh, he's down at the barn helping Dad with a chore. He said to tell you hi."

Seth grinned. "In that case, I'll let you tell him hello for me, too."

While she buckled her seat belt, Seth skirted the hood of the truck and slid behind the steering wheel. In a matter of moments they were headed away from the house and toward the setting sun.

As she settled more comfortably in the plush leather

seat, Seth asked, "What kind of chore is Matthew helping his grandfather with?"

His question brought a worried frown to Corrina's forehead. "Dad and Matthew tore off a pile of lumber from the barn last year and now Dad's decided to get energetic and burn it. I tried to talk him out of doing it tonight, but he's promised to keep the water hose close by."

Seth glanced her way and for a moment he forgot what he'd been about to ask her. She'd always been beautiful to him, but tonight she looked especially lovely. Her skin glowed like a creamy pearl and her fiery curls were gilded by the last golden rays of the sun. A fine silver chain with a small heart-shaped charm circled her neck and nestled in the faint shadow between the tops of her breasts.

Seth realized he wanted to touch her there in that soft alluring spot. With his hands and his lips. He wanted to kiss her mouth, and then kiss her some more. He wanted to hold her warm body next to his, feel the beat of her heart and smell the sweet scent of roses on her skin. For the first time in a long time, he wanted to make love to a woman.

Drawing in a deep breath, he focused his gaze on the road ahead and tried to push the provocative thoughts away. He couldn't take Corrina to his bed. She wasn't that kind of woman. She was the marrying kind. And he was…well, he was just a Texas Ranger.

"I thought Rube couldn't get around good," he commented. "I've seen how hard it is for him to walk for even a few short steps."

Corrina nodded. "Some days his knees are swollen and painful. But thankfully there are days when he has no pain at all."

"Then his condition isn't totally chronic," Seth said.

Corrina looked at him. "Well, yes. I'd say it was chronic. He's never going to get any better."

Not if he didn't try, Seth thought. And from all appearances, Rube did nothing to attempt to improve his health.

"Does he take prescribed medication?"

Corrina shook her head. "He swears aspirin is good enough for him. He went to see your sister two or three months ago for a barbed-wire cut on his hand. At that time, she tried to prescribe him an anti-inflammatory drug, but he told her she'd be wasting her time. He wouldn't take it."

"Hmm. Well, older people sometimes get stubborn about things," Seth reasoned.

"Dad's only sixty-five. That's not old."

The main county road came into view and Seth eased his foot off the accelerator. "No, that's not old," he agreed.

As he geared the truck to a halt, Corrina turned a thoughtful eye on him. "To tell you the truth, Seth, I don't know what's got into him."

It surprised Seth that she was discussing her father with him. So far she'd wanted to keep mum about Rube and about herself. It lifted his spirits to think she was sharing more of her personal life with him.

"What do you mean?" Seth asked.

She shrugged one shoulder. "Oh, it's nothing really. But this evening, when he was talking about cleaning up the barnyard, he also mentioned sprucing up the place, building a new barn and buying another horse to go with Blackjack."

Seth's eyebrows lifted. "Well, that's not so unusual,

is it? Matthew told me that you used to have another horse, but that your father sold him.''

Corrina nodded grimly. "Frankly, between you and me, it was because he needed the money. Not that he ever said anything like that to me, but I could read between the lines, if you know what I mean. And now…well, it's pretty obvious that other than his social security check, Dad doesn't have any means of making money. I don't know where he thinks he could come up with enough funds to buy a horse or build a barn.''

Seeing she was troubled by her father's sudden mood swing, Seth tried to make light of the whole situation. "Well, I wouldn't worry, Corrina. More than likely your dad is just doing some wishful thinking out loud. He probably would love to buy a horse for his grandson and, since he can't, talking about it is the next best thing.''

Corrina's heart suddenly warmed as she looked at the man sitting next to her. He could have used this opportunity to badmouth her father. Instead, he was trying to give her reasonable excuses. She was grateful to him for that.

"Yes, but that isn't fair to Matthew. He'll get his hopes up and then be disappointed when Dad doesn't come through with his promises.'' *The same way he'll be disappointed when you leave,* Corrina thought dismally. For some reason, her son believed Seth was going to remain in their lives forever and she dreaded the day when he would have to face the hard truth of the matter.

"Give your son a little credit, Corrina. He understands his grandfather better than you think.''

Her gaze dropped to her lap. "I hope you're right.

Matthew has been through a lot. I want—I want his future to be good.''

Seth glanced over at her bent head and something sudden and almost painful hit him deep in the chest. Corrina was a strong woman. For years she'd been providing for her son and herself without the help of a man or a family. Now she was seeing after her father, too. Her life couldn't be easy. Yet she never talked about wanting things for herself or wishing that she could make her own life better. And Seth wondered if she'd long ago given up on having a happy life for herself. The idea so saddened him that it was all he could do to keep from stopping the truck on the side of the road and pulling her into his arms.

Dear heaven, she was doing it again, Corrina thought with a sudden start. She was fretting, worrying like a timid old spinster.

Lifting her head, she cast an apologetic smile at him. "I'm sorry, Seth. You didn't ask me out tonight just to hear my problems. Sometimes I forget that I'm...supposed to be relaxing.''

He reached over and touched her arm. "It's all right, Corrina. I want you to talk to me about anything. Everything.''

The pleasure of his touch slivered down her spine and as her heartbeat quickened, her smile at him widened. "Okay. Where are we going to eat tonight?''

A sheepish look quickly spread over his rugged features. "Well, to be honest, I had planned to drive you up to Durango to a fancy restaurant, but then something my mother used to say made me decide differently. I hope she was right.''

Curious, she twisted her knees around so that she was facing him. "And what did your mother used to say?''

"That a woman doesn't need fancy. She just likes to know she's wanted."

Did that mean he wanted her? Maybe physically, she mused. The passionate way he'd kissed her told her that much. But he couldn't want her any other way. She was a Dawson. Dawsons weren't the sort to marry into a family like the Ketchums.

Yet even knowing all that, Corrina couldn't subdue the pleasure she felt at just looking at him, at knowing that he desired her.

"I...believe your mother was right," she said huskily.

He shot her a brief smile. "When we get to where we're going I'll see if you still think that way."

A few minutes later Seth pulled the truck through the T Bar K entrance and accelerated the truck up the winding dirt road that led to the house. Corrina was so surprised, she stared at him with wide eyes.

"We're going back to your ranch." She stated the obvious.

"That's right. Disappointed?"

She glanced around her. The sparkling river was on one side of the road, while on the other, small green meadows dotted with evergreens were full of fat, grazing Angus cattle. No matter how many times a person saw this ranch, it would always be beautiful, she thought.

"I—well, no," she answered him. "Just surprised, that's all."

He reached over and squeezed her hand. "I decided to do something special this evening. If you don't like it, we'll drive into Aztec and eat. All you have to do is tell me."

Corrina swallowed as a lump of emotion filled her throat. No man had ever been so thoughtful or considerate to her. And no man had ever made her heart turn over with just the touch of his hand.

Oh God, help me, she prayed. *I'm falling in love with this man.* With each passing minute, she could feel her heart going out to him, feel her senses falling deeper and deeper under his spell.

"I'm sure it will be very nice," she murmured.

When they reached the ranch house, Seth drove around to the back and helped her out of the truck. Once on the ground, she expected the two of them to walk to the back porch and enter the kitchen. Instead, he took her by the hand and led her around to the side of the house that was built adjacent to a rocky bluff. There in the yard, beneath two tall pines was a small table draped with a lacy cloth and set for two.

"Oh my!" Corrina exclaimed on sight of it.

Seth paused as he studied her reaction to the intimate setting. "What do you think? I'd hoped you might enjoy eating outside."

She looked up at him and he could see her eyes were sparkling in the waning sunset. "It's…just wonderful," she said, her expression clearly amazed. "But you shouldn't have gone to so much trouble, Seth!"

Her appreciation filled him with pleasure and mellowed his voice to a soft drawl. "Not at all," he said and urged her toward the table.

He took care in seating her, and after she was settled he quickly lit the cluster of candles sitting in the middle of the table, then moved beyond the table to light a couple of torches that would keep the insects away.

"Comfortable?" he asked.

She smiled at him while thinking she felt like a princess being courted by a gallant knight. It was a feeling she'd never experienced before and it almost made her giddy.

"Very," she said.

"Good. You sit right there and I'll go get our supper."

Before he could walk away, she asked, "Marina won't be serving us?"

He glanced over his shoulder at her and a wicked smile crinkled the corners of his hazel eyes. "Marina's gone home for the evening. She's left the serving to me."

Corrina suddenly found it difficult to breathe and her skin seemed to prickle with anticipation. To what exactly, she wasn't sure. She only knew it was dangerous to be here alone with Seth. But it was a danger she embraced.

For so long now she'd lived solely for her son and her father. Tonight was going to be for herself. And for Seth.

Short minutes later, Seth returned carrying a huge tray laden with several dishes and two tall glasses of iced tea.

She began to rise from her chair. "Here, let me help you," she offered.

Seth quickly motioned her back down. "No, you stay right where you are. I'm doing the work tonight. We're starting out with tossed salad, then moving on to rib roast, scalloped squash, candied carrots and fresh green beans. How does that sound?"

She laughed. "Like you have enough food to feed an army."

He placed the dishes on the table and then took a seat in the chair across from her. Corrina smiled as he lifted her hand from the tabletop and squeezed it. "Look out to your right, Corrina. Isn't that a beautiful sight?"

If she were being honest, she'd have to admit she'd rather look at him. Tonight, with his jeans, he was wearing a moss-green shirt with a button-down collar. Since his initial visit to her father's house last week, this was the first time she'd seen him in short sleeves. His arms were thick and corded and just as brown as his face. Growing up, she'd remembered him as being a tad shorter and a bit stockier than Ross and Hugh. Seth had developed into an even bigger man, she decided, and every inch of him appeared to be lean, hard muscle.

Thrusting that tempting thought aside, Corrina turned her head slightly away from him to look in the direction he'd suggested. The orange-red ball of sun had slid from the western sky and across the mesa, purple and pink shadows painted the spiny yuccas, prickly pear and choylla. A hawk soared close to the ground and then came to rest on a tall sphere of red rock. Beyond the mesa, in the far, far distance a range of dark blue mountains were capped with snow.

A soft sigh escaped her lips. "It's so peaceful, so lovely."

And so was she, Seth thought as his eyes glided over the blush on her high cheekbones, the faint smattering of freckles scattered across her small nose and the moist curves of her full lips. As a boy, he'd thought she was the prettiest thing he'd ever seen. Now, as a man, he was even more enamored of her loveliness.

"Then you don't mind us having supper out here?" he asked.

She turned her gaze back to him and in that moment she could feel the frozen fingers around her heart melting. No man had ever cared whether she was pampered or spoiled for five minutes, much less for a whole meal. How could she not feel good things for this man who'd taken pains to make her feel special?

A shy smile tilted her lips. "Your mother was right," she added. "Fancy isn't what this woman wants."

His hazel eyes met hers and she suddenly became aware that he was still holding her hand, and the look on his face said the cooling food was the last thing on his mind.

Her heart thudding in her chest, she cleared her throat and pulled her fingers from his. Reaching for her fork, she said in a husky voice, "We'd better eat. We don't want Marina's delicious food to get cold. And I am hungry."

Grinning, he motioned for her to fill her salad plate. "I'm glad. I'd hate to think I went to all this trouble for you to pick at your food like a bird."

She helped herself to a bowl of salad greens dressed in oil and vinegar. "Don't worry, I won't. I can't remember the last time I've had prime rib. And I've never eaten a meal by candlelight. Unless it was because the electricity had gone off during a storm."

He glanced up from his salad. "You're kidding."

A blush stung her cheeks as she slowly shook her head. "No. That's the truth."

He leaned back in his chair and studied her as though she'd just confessed to a sinful secret. "I've never heard anything so awful. A beautiful woman like you should've had lots of candlelight dinners."

Dropping her gaze to her salad, she said, "Dale wasn't a romantic man. And since him...well, I haven't exactly had very many dates."

She began to eat and he followed her example even though his thoughts continued to linger on what she'd just said. If she'd not had candlelight dinners, then more than likely she'd not had bouquets of roses or tulips or daisies. No doubt she'd not been given diamonds or rubies or any sort of sparkling gems that women adored to wear.

Maybe she considered all those things trivial but he didn't. It wasn't right, that she'd been neglected. Corrina was a good woman. A totally unselfish and giving woman. She deserved to have some man take care of her, shower her with gifts and most of all, love her.

The last thought hit him hard, and beneath his lowered lashes he studied her face. Was he crazy? He didn't want some other man touching her, much less *loving* her!

But you can't be that man, Seth. You know it would be a mistake for you to marry. You'd be asking too much of any woman to put up with the life you lead. And anyway, you've got to head back to Texas soon. No way would Corrina leave that daddy of hers. You don't even have to ask, to know that much.

"Then I'm glad I thought of this," he murmured almost in afterthought.

She smiled at him and Seth felt another stab of possessiveness hit him like a ton of alfalfa hay. He didn't know what in hell had come over him. When he'd agreed to come back home to the T Bar K to try to solve Noah's murder, he'd never expected to find himself getting soppy over a woman. Much less Corrina Dawson. But every time he looked at her, he got as soft as a marshmallow. And even worse, he didn't think the feeling was going to go away anytime soon.

"Tell me about your job," he urged after a stretch of silence had passed between them.

Corrina laughed softly as she pushed away her salad

bowl. "That's funny, Seth. You're the one with the interesting job and you want me to tell you all about being a waitress?"

He shook his head. "I'm not talking about your job at the Wagon Wheel. I can pretty much guess what being a waitress is like. I thought you said you worked as a teacher's aide in Aztec."

Impressed that he'd remembered, she nodded. "I do. And I like it very much. But I'd like it even more if I could be a teacher."

Seth's eyebrows perked with interest. "Really? I didn't know that sort of thing interested you."

Corrina nodded. "I know it probably doesn't seem like a lofty goal to you, but it's very important to me."

He began to pass her the prime rib and accompanying vegetables. "I think it's a very noble goal," he said. "So what are you doing about it?"

"Well, I was going to college at nights. I don't need too many more hours until I can get my degree in English. But since Matthew and I moved back here with Dad, I've had to put my studies on hold."

"Why?"

She grimaced as she sliced into the succulent beef. "Why? Because I—I have too many responsibilities. I just can't keep up with everything that needs to be done at home and work, too. And finances are tight."

"You're working two jobs. You can't do more. What about your father, can't he help you?"

She looked at him as though she questioned his sanity. "On a fixed income?"

He frowned as he milled fresh black pepper over the food on his plate. "Well, that doesn't mean he doesn't have some sort of savings. The man worked that ranch of his for thirty years and he told me he sold off his cattle not too long ago. He must have put some of his profit away for important needs. And I'd say helping his daughter further her education is pretty darn important.''

"Dad doesn't have any savings. Not that I know of.'' She looked at him, her expression vexed. ''You see why I got so disturbed when he started talking about buying a horse? I realize that everyone has to do a certain amount of spending for fun. But he doesn't think about the necessities and—'' She suddenly stopped and closed her eyes in embarrassment. ''Forgive me, Seth, I'm doing it again. And you didn't ask me to dinner just to hear me complain and gripe. I promise not to do it again.''

"You have plenty of reason to.''

She sighed. ''Maybe. But…I don't want you to think I'm a—well, a you-know-what.''

An amused look came over his face. ''I don't think you could ever fall into that category, Corrina.''

She released a nervous chuckle. ''I don't know. Dad called me a mother hen tonight. And believe me, I didn't like it.''

"Corrina, when are you—'' He stopped, realizing now wasn't a good time to ask her when she was going to see her father for what he really was. When was she going to face up to the fact that she was working herself to the bone for a man who didn't appreciate her efforts?

"When am I what?'' she prompted him to finish.

He smiled and shrugged. Maybe he was a coward, but he didn't want tonight to be spoiled and he didn't want to hurt her with words she would probably take to heart in the wrong way.

"Oh, I was just going to ask you when you thought you might be able to finish your studies.''

"I keep promising myself it will be soon." Determined to remain upbeat, she smiled at him. "I'll be making more money when my job at school starts up again this fall. I'm hoping I'll be able to enroll in a few classes then. As for Dad getting around and helping me with the chores, I'm going to do my best to get him to a doctor and on some sort of medicine to make him more comfortable."

By then he'd be back in San Antonio, Seth thought, and hopefully the mystery over Noah's murder would be solved. But what about him and Corrina? he wondered. He couldn't imagine going back to work and forgetting her. Hell, nearly twenty years had passed and he hadn't forgotten her. Not totally. And now he was beginning to really know her, to feel close to her. Closer than he'd ever felt toward any woman. How was he going to leave here knowing he wouldn't be able to see her, touch her, hear her voice?

Don't think about that now, Seth. Don't think about all the years you've lived alone without a wife or children. Without anyone to love except for a long-distance family.

"I hope so, Corrina. It's time you started thinking about yourself for once."

Surprise flickered in her eyes and for a moment he thought she was going to say something. Probably in defense of her father. But she didn't. Instead, she smiled and began to talk about the T Bar K.

"I've always wondered how you could leave this place," she said thoughtfully. "I thought…you'd probably stay around and help your brothers run the ranch."

A wry smile touched his lips. "That's what was expected of me. But I bucked my father's wishes and went into law enforcement."

"Was being a Texas Ranger something you'd always wanted?"

He nodded and she watched the expression on his features turn nostalgic. "My mother, bless her, seemed to always understand my fascination for the law. For my twelfth birthday, she gave me a book about the Texas Rangers. I was enthralled that in the early days of the association, the men had nothing but a shotgun or rifle and a good horse to help him patrol vast areas of wilderness. They were real men. Tough and brave. I knew I wanted to belong to that legacy."

Forgetting her food for the moment, she rested her forearms on the edge of the table and gazed at him with sincere interest. "I'm sure it was much easier to become a Ranger back then."

He chuckled and Corrina realized how much she loved the sound. It made her feel good. It made her believe there were things in her life to be happy about.

He said, "You had to be honest, physically durable and possess your own horse and weapon. Today you have to have a college degree and serve a length of time in state law enforcement before you can even attempt to get in the Texas Rangers. Then you vie against hundreds of men for one opening."

"So your mother supported your decision to become a Ranger?"

A wry smile touched his lips. "I didn't have Dad's blessing. But Mom was proud."

Moisture gleamed in her blue eyes as she smiled at him. "I'm proud of you, too, Seth. I'm proud to be your friend. I am your friend, aren't I?"

His head lifted and emotion, sweet and soft, filled his eyes as he looked at her. "Corrina, what am I going to do with you? Don't you know that—" He reached over and picked up her hand. "You *are* my friend. And more."

Her heart was beating so fast she could hardly breathe, and when he lifted her fingers to his lips, it was all she could do to keep from groaning out loud.

"Seth, I—"

"Don't say anything right now," he urged gently. "Not about us. Let's finish our supper."

He didn't have to worry. If she sat here for the remainder of the night, she wouldn't have known what to say to him. She wasn't even sure what *he'd* been trying to say to her. But just the implication that he thought of them as a couple was enough to shake the ground beneath her.

Chapter Eight

The remainder of the meal was finished with very little conversation. But Corrina didn't mind. She didn't need a lot of words from him. It was nice, oh so nice, just to be sitting here with him in the gathering darkness, the candlelight flickering in the warm night.

Several times he reached across the table and touched her hand, and each time she realized she wanted more from him. She wanted to slide her arms around him, snuggle her body against his and let the fire build between them. And there would be fire, she was certain of that, she thought recklessly.

"Would you care for dessert?" he asked, breaking into her carnal thoughts. "Marina made peach cobbler."

With an inward shiver, she looked at him and smiled. "I'm too full to eat another bite. But please go ahead and have some yourself."

He slid a hand across his midsection. "I couldn't eat another bite, either. Maybe we could sample it later," he suggested, and then rising from his seat he came around the table and reached for her hand. "Would you like to walk down to the barn and look at the horses?"

She placed her hand in his and allowed him to help her to her feet. "That would be nice. But it's dark," she pointed out.

He shot her an indulgent smile. "There are lights in the barn, Corrina. All we have to do is flip a switch."

"Oh." Her cheeks reddened as she pulled a face at him. "I guess it's pretty obvious what a hayseed I am. We, uh, never were well off enough to have electricity run to the barn."

"Quit apologizing," he scolded. "You couldn't help the circumstances you grew up in, no more than I could."

She watched him lean down and blow out the candles, then snuff the torches. Back at her side, he gave her a crooked grin and slid his arm around the back of her waist. "The ground is uneven," he explained. "I don't want you to stumble."

Corrina glanced back at the table. "What about clearing our dinner mess away? Don't we need to carry it into the house?" she asked.

He urged her forward in the direction of the ranch yard. "Don't worry about it. The scraps will give the coyotes a tasty dinner tonight."

She didn't doubt the small wolves would come this close to the house. Especially for a bite of delicious beef. The T Bar K was set back in the wilderness, without any neighbors or civilization for miles in all directions.

"They might break the dishes." She tried one last time to change his mind.

He chuckled. "If they do, I'll buy some more."

Just like that, she thought. To him, buying dishes was a trivial thing and the notion reminded her of just how far apart their worlds had always been.

The trek to the horse barn was short, but Corrina savored every moment of walking next to him and having his strong arm wrapped warmly around her. The feeling of being a part of his life, of being connected to him physically was something that would end and soon, she told herself. But while he was here, it was too sweet to resist. Especially to a woman who'd had very little attention or affection in her life.

When they reached the long shed row, Seth flipped a switch and a row of fluorescent lights flickered to life beneath an overhanging porch. Horses whinnied softly and stirred in their small quarters. Several heads hung over stall gates and turned curious gazes in Corrina and Seth's direction.

"Such beautiful animals," Corrina softly remarked as they made their way to the first stall and a red roan with a blaze down his face. The gelding nibbled at her hand and she glanced up at Seth. "I wish I had a treat to give him."

He patted the horse's jaw, then smoothed his forelock. "Believe me, the horses aren't hungry. Linc feeds them better than Marina feeds us. But they all like attention."

Just like a woman wanted attention from the man she loved, Corrina thought as she felt his fingers tighten against her waist. The notion unsettled her and she glanced at him from the corner of her eye. The man she loved? She couldn't *love* Seth! She couldn't love him, just because she'd carried a torch for him all these years. Just because he treated her with more respect than she'd ever been treated by any man or because her heart turned over every time she looked upon his face. To love a man that would never be hers would be begging for heartache.

Swallowing away the lump of unease in her throat, she did her best to focus on other things besides her scattered emotions.

"So Linc takes care of the horses?" she asked, trying to put a lift in her voice. "I didn't realize your cousin still lived on the T Bar K."

They paused at the stall of a black mare with a tiny star in the middle of her forehead. The horse immediately nudged Seth's shoulder and nosed at his shirt pocket.

"I'm not Linc, Mayblossom. I don't have any sugar cubes for you," he told the mare, then glanced at Corrina. "Linc oversees the breeding and training of all the horses, including the ranch's own remuda and those that we raise to sell. I don't know what we'd do without him."

"I always thought Linc was more like you than Ross or Hugh. It surprises me that he made ranching his life. I expected him to move away and become a lawyer or something like that. Did he ever marry?"

With a brief smile, Seth shook his head. "No. So I guess he is more like me than I thought."

Corrina stroked the black mare's velvety nose. "Hmm, I wonder why," she mused aloud. "Linc was always a nice-looking man. I'm sure he wouldn't have any trouble finding a wife."

Seth's hand slid up the middle of her back, then settled warmly over her shoulder. She didn't know how his touch could be so exciting and comforting at the same time. But it was. And she desperately wanted to lean back against him, to rest her head on his broad chest.

"I don't think Linc has ever wanted to find a wife," Seth told her. "I'm not exactly sure why. But his parents had a volatile marriage, and when they finally divorced, Linc had a lot of problems with the whole thing. I believe his feelings about marriage are connected to that. I guess he doesn't want to go through all that grief again. Not that the unhappiness ever ended for Linc. His mother still won't have anything to do with him."

A soft gasp of surprise parted Corrina's lips as she stared up at him. "Are you kidding?"

Seth grimaced. "No. That's nothing to kid about."

Stunned, she shook her head. "I can't imagine any mother deserting her child. But I guess it does happen," she murmured sickly.

He gently squeezed her shoulder. "No. A woman like you can't imagine it," he agreed. "Because your heart is too big. You could never hurt anyone."

Tilting her head back, she gazed up at him. "How could you be sure of something like that, Seth? We haven't seen each other in years. And even then we were just…acquaintances."

His expression softened as his hazel eyes glided over her face. "It doesn't take long to see what a person is like on the inside. Not if you stop to take a look. And I can see how you are with Matthew. You're devoted to him."

And I'd be devoted to you if things were different. And I had the chance to love you.

The sudden thought pierced Corrina like a sharp arrow and left a bittersweet ache between her breasts.

"Maybe I'm too devoted sometimes," she said quietly. "But he's all I have and likely all I'll ever have."

With his hand on her shoulder, Seth urged her on down the shed row. "Did you want other children?" he asked as they strolled slowly by the beautifully groomed horses.

Corrina sighed. "Oh, yes. But after Matthew was born Dale forbade me to get pregnant again. You can imagine what a crimp that put in our...sex life."

Stunned by her admission, Seth took her by the arm and stopped her forward motion. "Corrina, that's— well, it's hard to believe. Didn't you talk to him about having children before you were married?"

She smiled at him as though his question was infantile, as though, he, of all people, should understand how duplicitous people could be. "Of course I talked to him. And anything I wanted back then was fine. In fact, Dale made a big issue of wanting a large family. He'd grown up an only child and he expressed that he didn't want *his* children to go through the same loneliness. Or so he said," she added with a sarcastic snort, then followed it with a gusty sigh. "Seth, it sickens me now to think how gullible I was all those years ago. I should have seen that Dale was full of lies, that all he cared about was himself. To tell you the truth, I really don't know why he married me. Except that I—I was a challenge to him." She looked away from him as her cheeks reddened. "Because I wouldn't go to bed with him and he...was obsessed with having me."

His hand slid gently, soothingly against her bare arm. "And marrying you was the only way he could have you," he stated with a heavy dose of censure.

She darted a glance at him, then looked down at the hard-packed ground beneath their feet. "The whole

and turned in the direction of the house, Corrina noticed it had grown pitch-black. She clung to Seth's arm and gladly let him pick the way over the uneven ground.

As they walked, a companionable silence fell over them. Corrina was drinking in the closeness of his body and letting herself imagine how things might be if they were man and wife, walking across their own lawn, to their own house and bed. The happy, contented feeling that was in her heart right now would never end.

Suddenly her dreaming was interrupted as Seth stopped their forward movement and glanced over his shoulder. Puzzled by his action, Corrina looked up at him and tried to find his face in the dark. From what little she could see, his eyebrows were puckered together with a frown and he was listening intently for something.

"What's the matter?" she whispered, sensing the tension radiating from the tightening muscles in his arm.

"Nothing. I just thought…I'd heard something."

"You probably did. There're cattle milling about in the pens. And the men—"

"Are eating supper in the bunkhouse. That's why it was so quiet down at the horse barn. The hands have already finished their chores for the evening," he said in a hushed voice. He appeared to listen for a few more seconds, then shook his head in a dismissive way. "It was nothing."

Seth was a highly trained lawman. His ears and eyes were attuned to pick up anything unusual. He wouldn't say he'd heard something unless he was fairly certain that he had. Uneasy at the thought that someone might have been watching them, she gripped his arm even tighter as she stared back in the direction from which they'd just come. "But you thought it was something. Seth, what—"

"Corrina, Noah Rider was killed, shot to death on this ranch. I don't know who or where the murderer is right now. And until I do, I've got to be on guard. We've all got to be on guard around here."

Shivering at the thought, she turned back to him. "I understand. I—" She was suddenly interrupted by the not-too-distant howl of a coyote. The lonesome wail was the same as the night before and the sound touched something deep inside her and caused goose bumps to rise upon her arms. Instinctively, she edged even closer to Seth's side.

Seeing her troubled expression, he quickly took her by the hand and urged her forward. "Don't be scared, honey. Nothing's wrong. It's only a coyote."

She clutched his hand as they hurried the last few yards to the front porch. "But it sounded as though he was trying to say something. To you and me. I feel like…something bad is going to happen. I just know it," she said, stunned by her own premonition.

Seth ushered her through the door and into the living room where a small lamp was burning in one corner of the room. After he shut the door firmly behind him, he reached for Corrina who was waiting a few steps away.

"You sound like Marina with her omens and superstitions," he teased as he pulled her into the tight circle of his arms. "And I can promise you there isn't going to be one bad thing about tonight."

Not more than an hour ago, she'd promised him and herself that she'd quit worrying. She wanted to show him that she could stick to that promise.

"I trust you," she said softly, her cheek crushed against the middle of his chest.

"You'd better trust me, sweetheart. Because I could never hurt you. Not for any reason."

She tilted her head back and looked up at his shadowed face. The gentleness she saw there caused tears to sting her eyes and she was forced to swallow before she could utter a word. "Make love to me, Seth," she said simply.

Her plea elicited a groan deep in his throat and he bent and picked her up in his arms. As he carried her through the house, Corrina's arms clung to his shoulders, her face buried against the strong column of his neck. With each step he took, her heart thundered louder and louder in her ears.

What was she doing? Had she lost her mind?

For one second the little voice asking those questions sent a shot of panic plowing through her. But then she felt Seth's strong arms cradling her, supporting her against his chest, and she realized that making love with him was meant to be. It was a path that both of them had been set on and neither one of them could change it even they wanted to.

Inside the bedroom, he laid her gently on a soft, wide bed. Beyond, at the windows, the faint glow of a yard light filtered through the parted curtains and cast soft shadows over the two of them.

Immediately, Corrina began to untie her wrapped skirt, but he leaned over her and pushed her hands away.

"Let me do that. I'm supposed to be serving you, remember."

She smiled up at him and the sexy glitter she saw in his eyes was enough to make her whole body throb with anticipation.

"That was supper," she pointed out.

"Yeah," he whispered. "And this is dessert."

A soft chuckle parted her lips and he bent to kiss them as he untied her skirt and slipped it away from her long, silky legs. When it came to her top, she rose to a sitting position and held up her arms so that he could pull the stretchy T-shirt over her head.

Left with only a lacy bra and panties, she leaned back against the mattress and watched as he quickly removed his own clothing. As each garment fell to the floor, Corrina was treated to the sight of thick, muscled arms, wide shoulders and a broad chest that narrowed down to a lean, hard waist. Below his white boxers, his thighs bulged with strength, and from out of nowhere she suddenly remembered what a powerhouse he'd been on the football field.

The girls had flocked around him then, but he'd never seemed overly interested in them. Not like the other boys or his brother Ross. That had intrigued Corrina, but she'd never gotten close enough to ask him why. She'd been too afraid of rejection. Afraid she would fall so in love with him she'd never get over it. And now it appeared she hadn't gotten over him.

He slipped his thumbs in the waistband of his boxers and turned aside as he stepped out of them. But once he stepped back to the side of the bed, his erection was very evident and the sight of his desire filled her with all sorts of strong emotions. He wanted her! And the knowledge was so empowering to her femininity that she actually felt giddy.

"You really do want me," she said, her voice softened with an odd sort of wonder.

Placing a knee on the bed, he climbed up beside her. "I can hardly hide it," he gently teased.

She twisted onto her side and slid one arm around

his waist. As she gazed at his face just inches away, her heart pounded as though she'd been running. Running *from* something or *to* something. Either way, she was a little scared, a little dazed. "I can't believe I'm here with you like this," she confessed.

Thrusting his hands into her thick chestnut curls, he drew her mouth to his and nibbled at the sweet curves. "I've thought of making love to you many times," he admitted. "I just never believed it would come true."

She pulled her head back and stared at him in disbelief. "You dreamed about making love to…me?"

The back of his forefinger brushed against her soft cheek. "Why not? You're the most beautiful woman I've ever known."

But she was a Dawson, she almost said, but she managed to tamp the words down before they could spill out and form a wall between them. He'd tell her it didn't matter to him about her family tree or her poor past. Certainly it didn't appear to matter at this moment. And she had to believe this was more than sex to him. If she didn't believe it, she'd have to get up and walk away from him.

"Oh I'm sure you've had a line of beauties hanging on your arm down through the years."

The kiss he pressed to her lips was a little punishing and even more promising. "You not only think too much, you talk too much, too," he murmured against her cheek. "There hasn't been a line of women in my past. There hasn't been anyone that's made me feel like this." With a groan of pleasure he slipped his hands to her back and drew her forward until the front of her body was molded to his. "Come here, baby, and let me show you," he added in a thick whisper.

Corrina gladly surrendered to his hungry mouth and

the hot thrust of his tongue. In a matter of moments, she was consumed with desire and desperate to keep his lips on hers. His skin was flaming hot beneath her hands and she touched him everywhere she could reach. His shoulders and arms, his chest, the flat nipples circled with curly brown hair. Her fingers lingered there to explore and tease before they eventually moved to his muscled hip and hair-roughened leg.

At the same time, Seth was busy unclipping her bra and sliding her panties down over her hips. Once he'd tossed the pieces of lace to the floor, he turned his attention to her breasts.

They were round and firm, the centers puckered to rosy-brown nubs. The sight of their perfection caused his breath to lodge in his throat as he reached to touch her.

He took his time exploring the mounds with his hands before he finally dipped his head and took mindless pleasure in tasting, nibbling, suckling each nipple until she writhed against him and begged for him to never stop.

But he did stop and a new set of sensations began to wash over her as his lips found the valley between her breasts, then worked their way down the center of her midriff. He paused long enough on his path to lave her belly button with his tongue before his head dipped lower until his teeth were grazing at the mound covered with red-brown curls.

Gasping at his boldness, she thrust her fingers into his hair and pressed them against his scalp. "Oh, Seth, no! You can't!" she exclaimed in a voice choked with desire.

His amused chuckle was muffled against her flesh. "Why can't I?"

"Because I—because you—oh—ooh!" The air whooshed from her lungs as his tongue found the secret place between her thighs and slipped inside the moist folds.

The teasing movement drove her mad with longing and the next thing she knew she was crying out with uncontrollable pleasure, wrapping her legs around his back and lifting her hips toward the magic of his mouth.

Sensing she was near the breaking point, he cupped her buttocks with his hands and urged her to give in, to let herself experience everything he was trying to give her. And in a matter of moments an incredible joy spread through him as he heard her cries of fulfillment and felt the rhythmic contractions of her climax.

By the time he eased her back against the mattress, her head cleared enough to realize what had just happened and she groaned with a mixture of embarrassment and regret.

"Oh, Seth—I—I'm so sorry. I wanted to wait—but I—but you—I never—"

He stopped her apology by planting a deep kiss on her mouth. "Now, why are you sorry?" he asked, his lips curved with wry amusement. "It's not like you can't do it again."

"Again! Seth, I—"

The remainder of her words slipped away on a blissful sigh as his hands covered her breasts and his mouth found the curve of her throat.

"We're just now starting, my love."

My love. My love.

The sweet words echoed in her head as his knee spread her thighs and he entered her with one smooth thrust. And later, as passion spurred their movements and their bodies became slick with sweat and desperate for relief, she clung to the words like a lifeboat in a tossing sea.

Hours passed before Corrina was able to convince Seth that she had to get home before the night ended and her father and son found her missing.

Seth reluctantly agreed, but as she started to climb from the bed, he scooted up behind her and wrapped his arms around her waist.

"I don't want the night to end," he murmured against the smooth curve of her shoulder.

Corrina's head bent as reality came crashing at her like a rocky avalanche. "Neither do I. But I have a son and a job and a father to look after."

For long moments there was no reaction from him at all. Then finally he placed a kiss on the nape of her neck. "I'll get dressed so I can take you home."

As he climbed out of bed and reached for his clothing, Corrina swallowed hard and blinked as tears stung her eyes. Dear God, she couldn't cry now. He'd think this had all meant something to her. He'd think she expected things from him that he wasn't prepared to give. Her tears would embarrass him and mortify her. But she'd never slept with a man simply for the sake of having sex. And this time was no different. She didn't know how to act cool and nonchalant. She didn't know how to hide the bittersweet emotions choking her throat.

A few minutes later, she emerged from the bathroom dressed and ready to go. He noticed her face was pale and strained as she walked beside him to the truck, but he didn't comment on it.

He somehow sensed she was as shaken as he was

about what had transpired between them. Yet he realized not nearly enough time had passed for him to prod her about her feelings.

As for him, his head was still reeling with the generous way she had loved him. And it had been love, he told himself. The way she'd touched him, kissed him, held him as though she never wanted to let him go was unlike anything he'd ever experienced before. She'd not just been going through the motions of having sex with a man. He'd felt a desperate hunger in her, the same as he'd felt in himself.

Face it, Seth, you've fallen in love with the woman. And you want her to return your love. You want this thing with her to never end.

The realization rattled around in his head throughout the drive to the Dawson ranch and he kept wondering what his newfound feelings were going to mean to him and, if anything, to her. He couldn't see himself simply walking out of her life. That option wasn't even on the bargaining table now. But how would she react when he asked her to leave New Mexico behind?

At the Dawson house, he braked the truck to a stop and glanced over at Corrina to see a surprised expression on her face.

"Oh. I didn't realize we were already here."

She gathered up her purse from the floorboard and reached for the door handle. At the same time Seth reached for her.

"Not so quick," he drawled, his hand on her shoulder. "Are you working tomorrow?"

Nodding, she cast him a regretful smile. "The evening shift. I won't be off until eight tomorrow night."

"I'll be there."

Her lips parted as though she was going to say some-

Chapter Nine

"You can laugh if you want," Marina said the next morning as she carried a plate of scrambled eggs smothered in green chili sauce over to the kitchen table where Seth sat waiting for his breakfast. "But something bad is going to happen around here. And soon."

Seth wanted to laugh again, but as he glanced up at the older woman and saw that her mouth was stretched to a tight, forbidding line, he decided he'd better take a different approach rather than risk making her peeved at him.

"I'm a detective, Marina. You have to give me a reason to believe this prediction of yours."

She snorted as she placed the plate in front of him. "Because the coyote said so. Didn't you hear him last night? Puttin' up a howl like I haven't heard in a long time."

"Marina," Seth scoffed as he dug his fork into the

eggs, "coyotes howl out here every night. He or she was just calling to its mate. That's all."

Marina fetched a tortilla warmer from the cook stove and placed it near Seth's elbow. "Probably was," she said as she eased down in the chair kitty-corner from his. "He was probably howling 'cause he knows something is gonna come along and kill his mate."

Seth raised his head up from his plate to stare at her. "I don't know where you're getting an idea like that, Marina. There isn't going to be any coyotes killed here on the T Bar K."

She made a helpless gesture with her hands. "How do you know? A man was killed here. Wouldn't be any more trouble to kill a coyote. Wild creatures know these sort of things."

Seth frowned. For as long as he could remember, Marina had been superstitious and mystical. Amelia, his mother, had often become frustrated with the woman's predictions and unreasonable logic, but most of the time Tucker had played it straight with the housekeeper and appeared to heed her advice. Whether his father had actually believed Marina had special instincts about things, Seth didn't know.

"What makes you think you can translate what a coyote is saying?" he asked dryly.

Marina proudly drew up her broad shoulders. "Well, I'm part Navaho, remember, and part Apache, too. It's just in my blood. It comes natural to us."

Leaning back in his chair, Seth folded his arms across his chest and shot her an indulgent smile. "Now, Marina, if I remember right, your folks came directly from Chihuahua, Mexico."

Marina quickly shook her head. "Only my papa. When he came up here to New Mexico, he was very young and he married a woman from the Navajo Nation. I was born to her. But she died when I was small and he married someone else. Someone from the old country.''

Seth picked up a flour tortilla and went back to eating. ''Well, I've certainly learned something today.''

''Then you learn you need to listen closer to me.''

Picking up an insulated coffeepot, she topped off the dark brew in Seth's cup while he was thinking it was no wonder Ross was so spoiled. Marina had probably waited on him hand and foot just as she'd been doing for Seth since he'd been here. The idea put a wry smile on his face.

''This Señorita Dawson,'' Marina went on thoughtfully, ''I think you need to watch her close. Maybe this warning has something to do with her. She was here last night. And the coyote, he must have known.''

Seth's amused expression suddenly vanished. Corrina had been frightened last night, he recalled. Not so much by the idea that he'd heard something back at the horse barn, but because the coyote had howled only a few yards away from them. Dear God, could Marina be right? No, damn it! He was a Texas Ranger. He needed factual evidence. He wasn't into the paranormal! Besides all that, Corrina had nothing to do with the mystery of Noah Rider's murder.

But Corrina was now connected to Seth. And that was enough to put her in danger.

Trying to shake away the chill creeping over his skin, he took another sip of coffee.

Across from him, Marina looked around at the back door. ''Someone's coming.''

By the time Seth heard the knock, she'd risen from

her chair and was halfway across the room to answer the door.

Seconds later, Seth picked up the sound of his cousin's voice.

"Hello, Marina. I thought I'd come by and talk to Seth for a few minutes. Is he up?"

"Havin' breakfast," Marina answered. "You want some?"

"No thank you, Marina. I've already eaten down at the bunkhouse."

"Bet mine would have been better," she muttered at him.

Seth turned around in time to see Linc bend his head and place a kiss on Marina's cheek.

"I know it would have, but I figured Seth would get jealous if I showed up and tried to horn him away from the table." He eased a battered straw hat from his head and took a seat opposite Seth. "Good morning, cousin."

Seth greeted him with a grin. "What are you doing out so early and away from all those broodmares? Surely there's one about to foal."

Linc chuckled as he propped the hat on a bent knee. "Not this morning. The moon isn't full enough yet."

Seth groaned. "Not you, too."

Linc's eyebrows lifted as he looked down the table at Seth. "What do you mean?"

Shaking his head, Seth glanced pointedly at Marina who was busy fetching Linc a coffee cup. "Oh, nothing."

As the older woman served him, Linc said, "I heard from Ross last night."

Seth looked at him with interest. "I've been wondering why he hasn't taken the time to call. Guess he and Bella are having a big time down in the Caribbean,'' he mused aloud.

"So far,'' Linc replied. "He said he tried to call you last night but couldn't get an answer. He was a little worried, but I assured him everything was okay.''

A frown tugged Seth's dark eyebrows together. "I don't understand why he was worried. It's not like I haven't taken care of myself for a lot of years now.''

Shrugging one shoulder, Linc took a careful sip of coffee. "It's not that, Seth. He—uh, well, he's worried about the Rider case. He's afraid something is going to happen if the killer isn't caught.''

It was on the tip of Seth's tongue to ask him if he'd heard anything strange going on down at the horse barn last night, but he didn't. Linc already spent too much of his time with the horses. If he feared something or someone was snooping around them, he'd never go to bed and get any sleep.

"I really don't see it that way,'' Seth told him. "I think the killer is going to continue to lay low. He doesn't want to do anything that might tip the law in his direction. Right now he's thinking he'll never get caught.''

Linc shot him a troubled look. "Is he right?''

Seth shoveled the last of the eggs into his mouth and swallowed them down with a sip of coffee before he answered. "Not if I have anything to say about it.'' He settled back in his chair and glanced thoughtfully at his cousin. "I was going through evidence yesterday and discovered some interesting things. Noah was found wearing a denim jacket.''

"That wouldn't be unusual. At the time he was killed we were in early spring. Some days are still chilly.''

Seth nodded. "I remember how the weather is up

here. The jacket isn't the thing that has me wondering. It's the evidence that was found on it.''

"What was that?"

"Horsehair," Seth answered. "From two different horses. Some black. Some gray.''

"Hmm. Well, that wouldn't be all that unusual, would it? Deputy Redwing said Noah was working at a feedlot down in Canyon. He was probably riding a different horse every day. There would be all kinds of horsehairs on it. Unless he washed the jacket often.''

"Yeah, or could be those horsehairs got on his jacket the day he was murdered. It goes along with the theory that he rode into that arroyo with the killer. Do you know anyone around here with black and gray horses?''

Linc laughed. "Just about every rancher in the county."

Seth grunted. "That's what I was afraid of.''

"Corrina, I've never seen you acting so jumpy. What in heaven's name are you so nervous about?''

As Corrina untied the apron from her waist, she glanced over at Betty. The other woman had already changed from her uniform and had grabbed up her purse in preparation to leave the diner. The evening shift was finally over and it had been an unusually busy one with many late-summer tourists wandering through the doors for supper.

Corrina had a pocketful of tips to show for her hard work, but she was exhausted beyond words and the idea of driving all the way home was not a pleasant one.

You wouldn't have been so exhausted if you hadn't stayed up half the night making love to Seth.

Seth! Seth! She'd not been able to get him out of her mind for more than a minute all day long. And she certainly hadn't been able to forget that he was supposed to be meeting her here at the diner when her shift was over. He was probably already outside, waiting. Was he going to ask her to go back to the ranch with him tonight? she wondered. Just the thought of repeating last night, of experiencing the euphoric pleasure his body had given her was enough to heat her blood.

But if he did ask, she would have to turn him down, she firmly decided. No matter how tempted she was to spend more time with him, she couldn't behave like a young, single woman. She was a mother and she had responsibilities.

"I'm not nervous, Betty. Exhausted is more like it."

"You've dropped your purse three times in the last two minutes." Betty had been on her way out the door, but now she returned to Corrina's side and watched the younger woman apply a thin layer of coral lipstick to her lips.

"What are you doing putting on lipstick? Aren't you going home?"

Before Corrina could answer, Betty's eyes widened and a knowing smile spread across her face. "Oh, it's *him* again, isn't it?"

"What do you mean *him?* Who's him?" Corrina asked innocently.

Betty cackled like a happy hen. "Don't play coy with me. It's that Ranger, isn't it?"

"Maybe."

Betty snorted. "There's no maybe about it. You've got that look in your eye."

Corrina snapped the powder compact shut and dropped it into her shoulder bag. "What look? I don't look any different than I ever do."

"Uh-uh. There's a glow you get in your eyes when he's around. It happened the other day."

Corrina stepped around her and headed down a short hallway to the back exit of the building. Betty followed close on her heels.

"You're imagining things," Corrina told her.

"No, I'm not," Betty argued. "And why in the world are you trying to deny it?"

As they reached the door, Corrina paused to cast a frustrated look at her friend. "I'm not trying to deny it. I—I—well, maybe I am," she admitted with a weary sigh. "This idea of me glowing whenever I see Seth, it—it makes it sound like I'm in love with him."

Betty's wrinkled face scrunched up in a deep frown. "And what's wrong with that? I think it's the most wonderful thing that could happen to you. You're young and beautiful. It's about time you started living again."

Corrina groaned. "I wish it were that simple. But...I can't get serious about Seth. He'll be going back to Texas soon."

Betty threw up her hands. "Can't you travel the same highway he does? They let women like you live in Texas, too."

"Oh, Betty! You—" Corrina's words halted as she spotted one of the evening cooks walking toward them. "Come on, let's get out of here before they decide to put us back to work."

Outside, dusk was falling and the air was beginning to cool. Before Betty could restart their conversation, Corrina said a hasty goodbye to the other woman and quickly headed to her car that was parked in the shadows at the far end of the parking lot.

She was unlocking the door, when a pair of male hands appeared from behind and clamped a tight hold on her waist. Yelping with surprise, she twisted around to see Seth grinning down at her.

"Seth!" she scolded. "You scared me!"

He chuckled. "If you'd been thinking about me you would have known I was here," he teased.

Thinking about him! That's all she'd done since he'd walked onto her father's ranch days ago!

Pulling a face at him, she said, "And if you were a sweet guy, you would have warned me you were close, instead of sneaking up on me like that."

"Hmm," he drawled as he moved his hands to the small of her back and slowly drew her up against him. "I was giving you a lesson. Showing you how easy some evil character could have gotten his hands on you and carted you away."

The hard warmth of his body acted on her senses like a strong shot of brandy. Every muscle in her legs went limp and useless. A pleasant fog clouded her brain.

"Not here in this small town," Corrina argued gently as she flattened her palms on his chest.

"Anywhere, Corrina. It can happen anywhere. Just like the murder on the T Bar K."

"Is that why you have such dark things on your mind—you've been investigating the case today?" she asked.

His hands slid up and down her back and she realized how much she had missed his touch, how eager she was to be with him like this, with his strong arms circled around her.

"I've been trying. But mostly I've been thinking about you," he murmured.

Corrina started to respond, but another worker chose that moment to step out of the diner's back door and walk across the parking lot to a nearby pickup truck.

Seth quickly took Corrina by the arm and led her beneath the shadowy arms of a nearby tree so the two of them would be hidden from any passersby. Then resting his back against the tree trunk, he pulled her into his arms and cradled her face with both his hands.

"Honey," he murmured, bringing his lips down to her cheek. "I've waited all day for this, to hold you again."

His eagerness made her heart soar as he planted warm kisses at the corners of her lips and the soft line of her throat.

"Seth!" she gasped as his palms suddenly cupped the weight of her breasts. "This is—we shouldn't be doing this out here—in the open!"

"Why?" he murmured huskily. "No one can see us here."

"Yes, but—" The remainder of her words turned into a pleasurable groan as his lips found hers in a deep, hungry kiss.

Beneath her fingers, his starched shirt crackled and the faint stubble of his whiskers rasped against her soft skin as his cheek rubbed sensually against hers. He smelled like horses and hay and the outdoors, and the masculine scent combined with the taste of him to shoot straight to her senses. A heady fog quickly clouded her brain, until she was aware of nothing but his lips feasting on hers, his fingers kneading her breasts until they were tight, achy mounds of flesh.

"Come home with me," he mouthed against her ear.

A quivery breath rushed past her lips. Already she wanted him like nothing she had ever wanted before. It would be futile to try to hide the fire he'd suddenly built in her.

Regret laced her voice as she whispered, "I want to,

Seth. But I can't. I can't stay gone two nights in a row. Matthew—''

"I know," he interrupted with a weighty sigh. "It wouldn't be right for you to leave him alone like that. But your father—"

"Isn't much of a companion for him," Corrina finished. The thought momentarily cooled her ardor and she turned her back to him and stared out into the falling darkness. "Maybe we should talk about this now, Seth. Before we—well, I don't want us to make mistakes."

His hands curved gently over her shoulders and squeezed. "Corrina," he said softly, "don't tell me that you regret what happened last night."

Her heart wept as a bittersweet pain swept through her. If he told her goodbye tomorrow, at least she would have those precious memories. "No," she said quietly. "I don't regret one moment."

He heaved a sigh of relief. "Well, I haven't forgotten that you're a mother. And I'm not trying to take you away from Matthew. I just want a part of you, too."

The longing she'd buried for him all these years surfaced to merge with the tension she'd been feeling all day. Together they shattered something deep inside her, and before she realized what she was doing she whirled back to him and said in a reckless rush, "I want a part of you, too, Seth!" Then with an anguished shake of her head, she corrected herself. "No, that isn't right. I want more than a part of you."

As Seth slowly digested her words, his eyes widened and a joy like he'd never quite felt before rushed through him like a roaring river.

Reaching for her shoulders, he tugged her back in his arms. "Corrina, sweet Corrina!" He groaned against

the crown of her head. "Do you know how that makes
me feel? Just to hear you say that?"

Anguish twisted her insides into knots as she slowly
shook her head. "You don't understand, Seth. I'm trying to tell you—I'm trying to say that—" Closing her
eyes, she let out a long breath then muttered, "I
shouldn't have said any of this. And I've got to get
home. It's getting late."

She started to pull away from him, but he tightened
his hold on her shoulders. "Whoa, now. You can't go
like this. You need to do a little more explaining."

*He's right. He deserves more from me than my beat-
ing around the bush like some timid spinster.*

Lifting her head, she met his eyes and felt her heart
suddenly thump into overdrive. "All right, Seth. I do
want to see you. I want to be with you. I want to make
love with you. But I—you probably know by now that
I'm a practical woman. I understand that this—whatever
this thing is between us—can't go anywhere. And I—"

"Who said it couldn't?" he butted in.

Her mouth opened but nothing would come out.

Scowling, he went on, "I don't know about you, but
I didn't think last night was a one-night stand between
us."

She gasped and heat scorched her face. "I didn't either! I mean—well, it wasn't like you picked me up in
a bar. But still, I realize that—" she drew in a bracing
breath "—all good things must come to an end."

No! Not as far as he was concerned. And why did it
have to? There wasn't anything to really stop the two
of them from being together.

Only her son. Her father. And his job.

If they could make it around those obstacles, the rest
would be smooth sailing. But is that what he wanted?

Lifting his head, he stared into the darkness as his mind whirled with questions. He'd always figured he would never marry. In fact, he'd pretty much decided to live out the rest of his life as a bachelor. In his opinion, his father had made a lousy husband and Seth wasn't altogether sure that he could be a better one. Not with the demands of his job. But after last night something had happened to him. Corrina was a part of him now and he couldn't bear to think of life without her.

He looked back down at her. "This isn't going to end, Corrina," he said flatly. "Not if I can help it."

The resolution in his voice took her by surprise, plus the fact that he wasn't treating their night together lightly. But then she should have known that Seth wasn't a superficial man. The code he lived by, the goals and standards he'd set for himself were far different from those of Dale or even her father. He wasn't just a Texas Ranger. He was a good man. And the fact made the thought of losing him all that much harder for Corrina to bear.

Her hands slid longingly up and down his arms. "Seth, I don't know what it is you're thinking, but—"

"Don't give me any buts," he interrupted. "Just say you'll spend as much time with me as you can. And then we'll worry about the rest."

His fingers lifted to gently touch her cheek, then slowly they moved downward and his forefinger pressed against the quiver of her lower lip. She closed her eyes and had to fight back tears as she felt love for him pouring into her heart, filling it so full that her chest ached with the weight of it.

"All right," she said in a low, wobbly voice, "I do want to be with you. But what comes later…I'm scared, Seth. So scared."

Groaning, he pressed her head against his chest. "Last night I told you that I would never hurt you. Trust me, Corrina. I meant it."

Trust him, a little voice inside demanded.

It was a simple command. And of all people, he should be the one she could trust. But believing in Dale and then having that belief shattered had squashed her ability to trust in anyone, most of all herself.

"I—I have to go, Seth," she said, her words muffled by the folds of his shirt.

Placing his thumbs beneath her jaw, he tilted her face up to his and as his hazel eyes looked into hers, he caught the wet glisten of tears. The sight tore right into his heart. But right at this moment he knew there was nothing he could do or say to ease her anguish.

"All right," he said. "I'll let you go. But you *are* going to see me tomorrow, aren't you?"

She nodded jerkily, then drew in a deep breath and let it out. "Why don't you come over for supper. I'm off tomorrow so I'll have plenty of time to cook. And Matthew would love to see you. Come about six and I'll let you help me in the kitchen."

It wasn't the private time he wanted with her, but it was far better than nothing, he thought.

Pressing a kiss to her lips, he said, "I'll be there."

Their gazes locked for long moments before he reluctantly released his hold on her. Corrina stepped away from him and without the warm circle of his arms, she felt so chilled and lost that she actually shivered. But she hurried away to her car before she was tempted to reach for him and beg him to take her to his home, his bed.

Chapter Ten

The next afternoon Corrina was in the laundry room sorting through a pile of clothing when Matthew stopped at the open doorway.

"Hey, Mom, when's Seth comin'?"

Corrina didn't respond and he stared at his mother with troubled eyes. "Mom, is something wrong?"

The sound of Matthew's voice dipped into Corrina's deep thoughts and she glanced over her shoulder to see her son standing a few steps away from her, a heavy-duty frown on his face.

Stuffing the shirt she'd been holding into the washing machine, she reached for a jug of liquid detergent and poured a measured amount on the dirty clothes. "Nothing is wrong," she said as casually as she could. "What makes you think there is?"

He shrugged both shoulders and scuffed the toe of his boot on the worn linoleum. "Oh, nothin'. Except you've been staring off in space and frowning a lot. And I just asked you a question and you didn't pay any attention to me.''

Corrina shut the lid on the washer and swiped a weary hand across her forehead. She had been preoccupied today. And what woman wouldn't be when she had Seth staring back at her every time she closed her eyes? But in spite of her thoughts being dominated by the tough Texas Ranger, she'd tried her best to go through the motions of doing her normal chores. Apparently, Matthew had picked up on her absent state of mind.

"I'm sorry, honey," she apologized to her son. "I just have a few things on my mind. What was it you were asking me?"

"When's Seth comin'?"

She sighed. Once she'd broken the news to Matthew that Seth was going to join them for supper, that's all her son had wanted to talk about. Which wasn't a bad thing in itself. The boy had to talk about something. But she was still very worried about him becoming so attached to Seth. How would he handle it once Seth was gone? Dear God, how would she?

"At six. I've already told you that."

"Well, I forgot," Matthew mumbled. "What time is it now?"

Corrina glanced at the watch on her wrist. "It's only two o'clock. You have several hours to kill before Seth comes."

He frowned and swiped a hand through his blond hair. As Corrina watched him, she made a mental note to take her son to the barber this weekend. He was going to look like a sheepdog if he didn't get a haircut soon.

"It's boring out here with nothin' to do. I wish school was going on. At least then I could see my friends."

"I wish it were going on, too. And then I'd be back in the principal's office helping Mrs. Phelps instead of waiting tables."

"Waitin' tables ain't so bad. You get to bring home good food sometimes."

She shot him an indulgent smile. He always ate like a horse, but very little extra weight showed on his frame. The fact that he was so thin used to worry her until about a year ago and she'd taken him to see Dr. Hastings. Seth's sister had assured her that Matthew was a very healthy boy. He was simply growing up in height so quickly that his weight couldn't keep up.

"You would consider food important."

Matthew's face brightened as another thought hit him. "When can I go see Aaron again? We could ride horses or hunt hawk nests."

"Maybe soon. If you're invited again."

He appeared to mull that over before he directed another question at her. "Can I go fishin' down at the stream? If I could catch enough trout we could have it for supper!"

The stream was hardly more than a yard wide and knee deep, but there were trout in it and she trusted Matthew to behave in a safe manner.

"All right. But don't stay down there all afternoon. I have some chores for you to do here in the house later on."

Matthew was so glad she'd given him permission to go fishing, he didn't stop to argue about the upcoming chores. He rushed out of the house as if there was a fire behind him, and a few minutes later, as Corrina stood at the kitchen window, she spotted him walking toward the west pasture with his rod and reel and Cotton trailing at his heels.

Suddenly out of nowhere a lump of tender feelings filled her throat and she had to blink several times to prevent tears from pooling in her eyes.

What in the world was wrong with her? It wasn't like her to get so emotional over nothing.

Stepping over to the table, she sank into one of the chairs and dropped her face into both hands. Who was she trying to fool? She didn't have to wrack her brain to figure out that Seth had a grip on her, both mentally and physically.

Since she'd left him last night at the diner parking lot, she'd pored over every word he'd said to her. And she still wasn't quite sure what he'd meant by any of them.

This isn't going to end. Not if I can help it.

With a tiny groan, Corrina pressed her fingertips against her closed eyes. Those words had sounded so permanent. Yet he couldn't have meant them. Not really, she mentally argued. He'd already told her he wasn't interested in taking a wife. And she certainly wasn't wife material. Not for a Ketchum.

So what did that leave? she asked herself. A long-distance affair? A few days together now and then, whenever he had the chance to travel to New Mexico? She couldn't do it. That sort of life wouldn't be fair to her or to Matthew. She wanted something better for both of them. She wanted a real family. She wanted love. Something she'd never had.

You have love now, Corrina. You love Seth. You always have. That won't ever change.

The little voice in her heart caused the lump of tears to re-form in her throat and she swallowed convulsively and wiped her eyes. Maybe she did love Seth, but that didn't mean he would ever love her back. She'd be foolish to ever hope for that much.

"Corrina? Corrina!"

At the sound of her father's call, she jumped up from the chair and hurried out to the back porch where he'd been sitting for the past hour with his beer and cigarettes.

"Yes, Dad. I'm here. Did you need something?"

He turned his head to glower at her. "Where the hell is that boy going?"

Even though her father could be contrary, it wasn't like him to use curse words with her. Especially when they were discussing Matthew.

Slowly, she stepped toward him. "You mean Matthew? He's going down to the stream. He wanted to do a little trout fishing."

He was silent for long moments and Corrina watched with dismay as his face turned beet red.

"What's the matter, Dad? There's nothing wrong with Matthew going fishing. He loves it and it gives him something to do."

He grabbed the arms of the lawn chair and made a move to rise up, but halfway to his feet he let out a painful groan and crumpled back onto the seat with a heavy thump.

"Damn it, just what kind of mother are you?" he asked between huffs and puffs for air.

Stunned, Corrina stared at him. "I like to think I'm a good one," she said simply.

"You must not be or you'd be worried the boy might drown himself!"

Anger spurted through her. "Drown himself! Dad, there's hardly enough water in that stream to wade in!

And Matthew is not a baby. He's old enough to do a little exploring on his own. It's good for him. It's part of growing up.''

Snorting, Rube waved a flustered hand in the direction Matthew had taken. ''Well, that's just it. He might not just go where he tells you he's going. He might wander off and get lost.''

Corrina's eyes narrowed as she carefully studied her father's agitated face. Rube had never once complained about where Matthew walked around on the ranch. For the life of her, she couldn't understand this sudden concern.

''We've lived here for more than two years and he's never gotten lost. But that's not what's bothering you,'' she argued. ''What is it, really?''

He expelled a long breath and reached for his beer can, but he didn't take a drink. Instead, he stared out at the barns that were still waiting to be repaired. ''I guess I'm just cranky because I can't do nothin','' he muttered.

As she watched the anger drain out of his face, she wondered if all this bluster was because he was feeling a little ignored. She'd had to work so many hours at the diner lately, and then her spare time had been taken up with Seth. The notion that her father might feel neglected made her realize how needy Rube was, and how lost he would be if she weren't around.

Leaning over him, she patted his forearm. ''You got out the other evening and worked burning the woodpiles. It looks real nice, too.''

''Yeah,'' he grumbled, ''but just doing that much has laid me up. My bones ached all day yesterday.''

Corrina hadn't noticed him complaining of pain yesterday. In fact, there were times she wondered if her father really experienced any sort of pain or simply used it as an excuse to sit and brood.

She eased down in the chair next to him. "I'm glad you brought this subject up, Dad. I want you to go see Dr. Hastings about your arthritis. She'll prescribe you something that will take away the pain and make your joints work better."

"No! I ain't goin' to no doctor. And that's final."

Frustration was threaded through her sigh. "You're not going to ever feel like doing anything unless you treat the problem."

He looked away from her and scowled. "I said no, daughter. Now don't press me."

Corrina mentally counted to ten and reminded herself to be patient. "Dad, are you upset that Seth is coming over for supper?"

Rube jerked his head around and stared at her in surprise. "Why no, honey."

"Well, if you are, I can ask him not to come. If you're not feeling up to company, I'm sure he'd understand."

All of a sudden Rube's expression turned apologetic and with a crooked grin, he leaned over and patted his daughter's cheek. "Now don't you go thinking about anything like that. I'm real glad Seth is comin'. Real glad. He's just the right man for my little darlin'. I always knew he was."

She closed her eyes and muttered, "Oh, Dad."

"What's the matter?"

Seth wasn't her man, she wanted to say. But the idea seemed to make her father happy, so she simply opened her eyes and smiled at him.

"Nothing, Dad. Not a thing. I'd better get to work and finish my chores."

* * *

At fifteen to six, Seth drove up the dirt road toward the Dawson house. As he approached the house, he could see Matthew jump down from the doghouse and run out to the flat area of the yard where his mother's and grandfather's vehicles were parked. By the time Seth pulled in beside the other vehicles and killed the engine, Matthew was standing at the driver's door with Cotton by his side. The white dog was barking and rearing wildly on his back legs.

Matthew hurriedly scolded his pet. "Hush, Cotton! Seth is a friend!"

Seth grinned at the two of them. How innocent and simple those days had been when he'd been Matthew's age, roaming the T Bar K with his dog and his horse. The only problem he'd had was keeping Ross away from his pellet rifle.

"He'll remember me in a minute," Seth assured the boy as the dog sidled warily up to his leg. He bent down and stroked the collie's head.

"Hi, Seth! Mom told me you were comin' so I've been watching for you."

Seth reached to shake the boy's hand and then patted him affectionately on the shoulder. Matthew beamed a wide grin up at him and Seth couldn't miss the happy sparkle in the boy's eyes. To know that Matthew liked him and looked up to him was more than gratifying. It filled him with a protective pride, a fierce possessiveness he'd never felt before. He wanted to gather Matthew under his wing, assure him he would always be loved and guided and sheltered.

Seth wanted to be Matthew's father. It was that plain and easy in his mind. But somehow he knew it wouldn't be so simple to Corrina.

"How are you, Matthew? Been keeping busy?"

Matthew continued to grin as he swiped at the hair flopping into his blue eyes. "I've been real busy today, Seth. Guess what we're gonna have for supper?"

Seth made a show of pondering the boy's question. "Oh, I don't know, probably pot roast."

Matthew's eyes sparkled. "No. Not that. Something better."

"Hmm. Must be fried chicken or spaghetti."

Clearly pleased at stumping him, Matthew said, "Well, that stuff is good. But this is even better!"

Pulling off his Stetson, Seth slowly scratched the top of his head. "You've got me, Matt. I guess I'm going to have to give up."

Matthew drew up his shoulders. "It's trout! And I caught all of them!"

Seth looked at the boy with real surprise. "Well now, I didn't know you were a fisherman, Matthew."

"Yeah, Mom taught me how a long time ago. And Pa helped me clean 'em. She's getting 'em all cooked up now. Come on and look!"

He followed the boy into the house and straight to the kitchen. Corrina was standing at the gas range with her back to them. Her mass of chestnut hair was pulled into a ponytail at the back of her head. A pair of snug blue jeans hugged her curvy behind and long legs and a simple white tank top served as her blouse. Seth couldn't help thinking that she looked delicious. As delicious as the smell of the frying trout.

"Mom, Seth is here! I brought him in!"

Corrina turned away from the stove to see Seth and her son standing in the middle of the kitchen. The room, which was already hot, got that much hotter as she drank in the sight of the man who'd become her lover.

Like her, he was dressed casually in blue jeans. He also wore a short-sleeved shirt of tiny blue print on a white background. His cream-colored Stetson was held at his side and she noticed his brown wavy hair looked as though it had been finger combed away from his face. He looked so strong and masculine, so dear and familiar that she wanted to run to him and greet him with a kiss as though he was her husband. The husband she'd always wanted.

"That's good, Matthew. You were supposed to bring him in," she said with an indulgent smile for her son before she focused her gaze on Seth. "Hi, Seth."

"Hello. I'm not too early, am I?"

Their eyes met in a long, searching glance and Corrina realized that no matter how much she'd tried to protest their being together last night, she was well and truly lost to this man.

"Not at all. I can put you to work," she told him.

He walked over to where she was standing and once he was at her side, he bent his head and placed a lingering kiss on her cheek.

"I'm a good cook," he murmured. "Have I told you that before?"

Flustered that he would display such open affection in front of her son, she glanced at Matthew who was standing nonchalantly at the corner of the dining table. The wide grin on his face told her he'd seen the kiss and was very happy about it. Oh dear heaven, she thought. Just another reason for Matthew to believe Seth wanted to become a part of their lives.

Breathing deeply, she lifted her face to Seth and though she tried to keep her expression prim and proper, the corners of her lips curled upward. "No. You haven't told me you could cook, good or otherwise. But your cooking skills aren't going to be needed tonight. I have everything nearly done. You can help Matthew set the table and put ice in the glasses.''

''Yes, ma'am.'' He walked over to Matthew and slung an arm around the boy's shoulders. ''Let's get to work, Matthew, so we can eat some of that trout of yours.''

Ten minutes later the four of them were sitting around the table eating fried fish, baked beans, steamed new potatoes and corn on the cob.

''I sure am glad you decided to go fishing,'' Seth told Matthew, then turned his gaze on Corrina who was sitting directly across from him. ''I haven't had trout in ages and this is delicious, Corrina. You're wasting your time waiting tables at the Wagon Wheel. You should be doing the cooking. They wouldn't have enough seating.''

''She learned that from her ma,'' Rube spoke up. ''Janie could make a bowl of scraps taste like a gourmet dish.''

Seth focused his attention on Corrina's father who was seated at the end of the small table. Rube had obviously spruced up for Seth's company. His plaid shirt was clean and his sparse hair was combed straight back from his forehead. For once, his face wasn't red or his eyes bloodshot. He was more like the Rube that Seth used to remember visiting the T Bar K back when Rube and Tucker had been much younger men.

''I don't think I ever met your wife, Rube,'' Seth commented. ''Did she look like Corrina?''

''Like two peas in a pod. Pretty as a June mornin'. God, it's still a shock to think about her keeling over like she did. I'd give anything—this whole place,'' he said, waving his arm in the general direction of the land around them, "just to have her back."

From the corner of his lashes, Seth could see a shadow cross Corrina's face before she bent her head. As for Rube, he had a vacant, wistful look in his eyes that told Seth the old man lived more in the past than he did in the present.

"I'm sure you would," Seth murmured. "Material things don't mean much compared to a loved one."

Rube rubbed a hand over his face and once he allowed it to fall away, Seth caught a glimpse of moisture pooling in the old man's eyes.

"Janie never had much. I tried to give her nice things, but it never worked out that way. She died before I could accomplish much. And then—I'll be honest with you, Seth, I just didn't care what happened to this ranch." He looked down the table and smiled crookedly at his daughter. "But that's all changed now that my girl is back home. She gives me something to live for. Her and Matthew."

Feeling more than awkward with her father's sentimental display, Corrina cleared her throat and quickly changed the subject. "So what did you do today, Seth? Help Linc with the horses?"

Seth shook his head. "No. I drove over to Bloomfield. The livestock auction was going on today and when Ross is home, he always makes a trip over there to see if anyone is trying to pass Snip through the sale ring."

"You didn't see him?"

Seth shook his head. "Unfortunately, no. But I bought a little paint filly just weaned from her mama."

"What are you gonna do with her?" Matthew wanted to know.

"Have her shipped to my ranch near San Antonio. Then when she grows up, she'll have some pretty babies."

Rube suddenly snorted. "Guess they don't have good horseflesh down in Texas."

Seth grinned. "Yes, sir. They do. But I fell in love with this filly at first sight. And when that happens, there's not much you can do about it but take her home with you."

He glanced across the table to Corrina and winked.

Her face turned crimson with heat, and pain burned its way from her stomach to her throat. Maybe he could make light of falling in love, but she couldn't. Not when her heart was spilling over with love for him. Not when it was aching at the idea of their time together ending.

"Well, I guess I can understand that," Rube remarked. "But this idea of yours and Ross's to look for Snip—hmmp—like I told you, son. That stallion is dead."

"We looked for him when we went riding on the T Bar K," Matthew spoke up.

Rube frowned at his grandson. "You didn't find him either. And you won't. He's been gone too long."

Seth watched as Rube went back to eating and he wondered why the old man kept insisting that Ross's stallion had met his end. Did he know something about the horse that he wasn't telling? Seth couldn't imagine it. As far as he knew, Rube rarely ever got off the place. But he could have overheard talk in the diner. Or an old crony might have mentioned the whereabouts of the horse to Rube. But if that were the case, Rube would have come forth with the information. He might be cantankerous, but he and Tucker had been friends. They'd argued over a racehorse, but Rube had insisted the two men had put all that aside.

Matthew quickly swallowed a mouthful of food. "Well, I promised Seth I'd keep an eye out for Snip," he said importantly. "And I will. If I find him, I'll rope him and bring him here to the barn. That way he couldn't get away."

Rube stared aghast at his grandson. "Don't you go doin' a dang-fool thing like that! Why, you couldn't handle a stallion, boy! He'd have you and Blackjack tromped to the ground!"

Corrina laid a hand on her father's forearm. "Dad, you're getting all worked up," she warned gently. "And for nothing. Matthew isn't going to run onto Snip. Like you said, the horse is probably dead. Now calm down and eat."

Rube looked at his daughter and then cut a sheepish glance toward Seth. After a moment, he let out a long breath and picked up his fork. "Yeah, yeah, you're right, daughter. Guess I got carried away."

Rube's blustery words didn't make much of an impression on Seth, but he couldn't help but notice as the old man lifted a bite of food to his mouth that there was a slight tremble to his thick hand. Rube was getting sick. Or, more likely, he had the shakes, Seth thought grimly. Rube had the trembles because he'd gone a few hours without any alcohol in his system. Either that or he was worried, terribly worried about something.

Suddenly it hit Seth with a clarity that shocked him. Rube was playing some sort of deception with them. He knew something about Snip and had known it for a long time. But what and how? And how could he pull the information out of the old man without making Corrina angry with him?

Deciding the supper table wasn't the time or place, Seth made a point of changing the subject, and from the look of relief on Corrina's face, he knew she was glad to get her father off his strange ranting and ravings about the lost horse. They finished the meal with small talk about the weather and the local happenings around Aztec and San Juan County.

Matthew was the first one to excuse himself from the table, and as he rose to his feet, he looked eagerly to Seth. "Wanta come with me to feed Blackjack?"

Seth glanced at Corrina who was finishing the last of the food on her plate. "Well, I was going to help your mother with the dishes," he told the boy. "But she can forget the dishes and come with us, don't you think?"

"Sure thing!" Matthew practically shouted.

"Oh, no," Corrina quickly spoke up. "This place is a mess. You two go on."

Rube shot his daughter a disgusted look. "Corrina! What's the matter with you, girl? You got company. Forget the kitchen and go on," her father argued. "I'll start putting things away here."

"Your knees—" she began, only to have him interrupt sharply.

"My knees are a damn sight better than your manners. Now get gone!"

Seeing she couldn't argue with the three of them, Corrina allowed Seth to help her to her feet. As she followed him and Matthew out the door, Seth said in a teasing voice, "I guess he told you."

Corrina sighed as a tiny frown wrinkled her forehead. "Seth, I don't know what's getting into my father. He's been acting so…strangely the past week or two."

As they walked toward the barn, Seth curled his arm around the back of her waist. Matthew chose to race ahead and climb up on the fence to wait for the slower-paced adults.

"Maybe I'm the reason," Seth carefully offered. "I understand Rube and Tucker were friends, but they also had their share of cross words down through the years. Your father might not like you seeing a Ketchum."

A wry expression crossed Corrina's features. "It's not you. He thinks you're just about the grandest thing to come along since sliced bread."

The compliment put a smug look on his face. "Hmm. It would be awfully nice if his daughter thought that, too."

She looked up at him and smiled. "I do think you're pretty grand, Ranger Ketchum."

Grinning down at her, he squeezed the side of her waist. "I'll remind you of that whenever we're alone tonight," he murmured wickedly.

They weren't going to be alone tonight, Corrina started to inform him, but Matthew chose that moment to call out to Seth.

"See his mane, Seth? I've been brushing it every day and it's gettin' longer and longer."

As the two of them approached the wooden corral, Seth said, "Blackjack looks mighty pretty, Matthew. I can see you've been taking good care of him."

Matthew beamed with pride. "Pa buys him high-protein feed. He says that will make his hair shiny and his muscles strong."

"Your pa is right," Seth replied.

The black horse trotted away from the fence and stood pawing at an empty feed trough sitting in one corner of the corral.

"I'd better go get his grain," Matthew said and quickly climbed down from the fence.

As the boy went into the barn to fetch a bucket of sweet feed, Seth looked at Corrina. "Thank you for inviting me over tonight."

He sounded so truly sincere, so grateful that her heart melted right then and there. "Thank you for coming," she replied.

His hand slid in a seductive up-and-down motion against her back. "I want you to know I haven't had much more than an hour's sleep since I saw you last night. We have to talk, Corrina."

Her gaze dropped to the toes of her sandals. "We did plenty of talking last night," she murmured.

"Not in my opinion," he retorted in a low voice.

Matthew emerged from the barn door and walked a few yards away from them to the feed trough. Not wanting her son to overhear any intimate words between her and Seth, Corrina didn't make any sort of reply.

Seth must have felt the same way, because he moved away from her and went to stand outside the fence where the horse was already busy munching the molasses coated oats and corn.

"I'll bet you really love your Pa for giving you such a nice horse."

Matthew joined Seth on the outside of the fence. "Yeah," he said, "but sometimes I get kinda mad at him. Especially when he drinks a lot of beer and hollers at Mom. But he's mainly good to me."

Seth turned his head slightly to see Corrina was walking over to join them. As he watched her, he couldn't help thinking that she more than deserved a special gift. She deserved love and a family. She was worthy of a husband who would protect and care for her the rest of their lives. Could he be that husband? he asked himself. He didn't know a whole heck of a lot about women.

His life had been the law and enforcing it to the letter. But he could learn how to be a husband and a father, he mentally argued. He had to learn. Because he couldn't envision his life without Corrina in it.

Chapter Eleven

The three of them lingered a few more minutes by the corral fence as they watched Blackjack enjoy his evening meal. After a while, as the sun began to totally disappear behind a low ridge of mountains, Corrina suggested she get back to the house to clean the kitchen.

"Pa's doing that, Mom," Matthew quickly reminded her. "You stay outside with Seth. That way you two can be alone."

She stared in stunned fascination at her son. "Matthew—"

"Take her for a walk, Seth," Matthew quickly interrupted his mother. "Girls like that. And give her a kiss, too!"

Pointing a finger at the grinning boy, Corrina firmly scolded, "All right, Matthew, you are in trouble now! You're not leaving this yard for two weeks!"

Laughing, Seth took her by the arm and began to lead

her away from the corral. "Don't worry, Matthew, I'll get her to relent," he called back to the boy.

"What in the world is going on around here?" Corrina muttered the question as she allowed Seth to lead her onto a dim path that trailed between stands of pungent-smelling piñon and juniper. "First Dad and now Matthew! They're both acting totally out of character."

"Matthew seems very happy," Seth commented casually.

"He is," Corrina blurted back at him, "and that's what worries me."

Seth paused to gesture at the trail in front of them. "Where does this go?"

It took Corrina's mind a moment to switch gears from her son's outrageous behavior to Seth's simple question. She touched fingertips to her forehead as she answered, "To the stream. Where Matthew caught the trout."

"Sounds nice." He slipped an arm around her shoulders. "We'll keep walking."

As he urged her forward, he asked, "Why should it worry you that Matthew is happy? Isn't that what you want for your son?"

She sighed. "Of course. But—he's—well, all this excitement he's showing is because of you. And I—"

"Look, Corrina, I think you're giving me way too much credit here. I'll bet that Matthew has always been a generally happy boy."

"Well—yes," she reluctantly admitted, then placing both hands on his arm, she tugged him to a stop. "But not *this* happy or excited about things."

Emotions he'd never experienced before slammed at Seth from all directions. To think he might be responsible for a child's happiness was scary and wonderful at the same time. And though he'd not pictured himself with children, he could easily imagine himself guiding Matthew through his teenage years. Moreover, he could envision Corrina growing great with his child. Not once, but two or three times.

"Corrina, I think the world of Matthew," Seth said to her gently. "I wouldn't hurt him for anything."

"I know. But he—"

She couldn't go on with what she'd been about to say. All of a sudden, she realized she didn't want to talk about his leaving. It hurt too much and the evening had been too pleasant to ruin it by hashing out something that couldn't be changed.

He looked down at her with a puzzled frown. "He what?"

Shaking her head, she dropped the clamped hold she had on his arm and began moving forward on the trail. "Nothing," she answered. Then reaching for his hand, she urged, "Come on, we can make it down to the stream before it gets dark."

The two of them walked together, hand in hand along the stony footpath that meandered through clumps of sage, century plants and tall outcroppings of red rock. Soon the trail took on a downward slope and before long the area opened up to a small valley dotted with cottonwoods and pines.

"We must be nearing the stream, I'm beginning to see green grass," Seth remarked.

Through the dusky twilight, Corrina pointed at a line of pine, willow and cottonwood trees. "There," she said. "Where the trees are thick."

They carefully picked their way along the stream where the overhanging tree branches shadowed the grass that grew like a thick green carpet along the banks. The shallow water gurgled and tinkled over boulders big and small and joined the sound of the wind in the pines to create a softly muted song.

Seth stared all around him with undisguised pleasure. "What a beautiful place. If I was Matthew I'd be down here every day."

"He does come often," Corrina admitted. "I think it's one of the nicest spots on the ranch."

Spotting a large willow standing at the water's edge, Seth led Corrina over to the base of the tree trunk and pulled her down beside him on the soft grass.

He was stretching out his legs and crossing his boots at the ankles when he noticed several horse tracks indented into the soft ground.

"Hmm. Looks like a horse has been visiting the stream," he commented thoughtfully.

Corrina gave the tracks a cursory glance. "I'm sure they belong to Blackjack. Matthew rides him down here."

"Did he ride him today?"

Corrina shook her head. "Not today. Why?"

Because the tracks were fresh, and from the looks of them the horse had lost a couple of shoes, maybe even three, Seth thought. He was certain Matthew's horse was wearing shoes on all four feet. But he kept the observation to himself. It used to be that Mustangs still roamed the mountains and the mesas around here. As far as Seth knew, there still might be a few wild ones in the area. He'd ask Ross later. Right now the last thing he wanted to think about was Snip.

"No reason. Just curious," he said. A slow, wicked grin spread across his face as he reached to pull her into his arms. "Come here and let me show you how much I've missed you."

As Corrina's upper body settled against his, he removed his hat and bent his head down to hers. With the nearby sound of the tinkling water in her ears, she closed her eyes and opened her mouth to his kiss.

The contact between them created instant combustion and in a matter of moments his lips were hungry and demanding and Corrina's mind swirled in a pleasurable fog as she clung to his broad shoulders.

"Corrina, it seems like weeks have passed since we made love," he whispered fiercely against the curve of her shoulder. "Do you know how much I've wanted you? How much I want you now?"

She shivered as heat zipped along her veins and throbbed at the very core of her womanhood. "I'd be lying if I said I didn't feel the same way," she murmured.

He moved his head so that his lips were able to press tiny kisses along her jawline and nibble at the sensitive spot behind her ear. "We need to go to the ranch where I can make love to you in my bed. That would be heaven!"

The image of his huskily spoken words were almost as erotic as the movement of his hot mouth against her skin and she groaned in response. "No. We can't, Seth."

His urgent lips moved onto her chin. "Why?" he gently demanded.

Her breaths grew short and jerky as desire began to build inside her like the slow, burning pressure of a cook pot. "Because—it—it would look too obvious," she managed to choke out. "It has to be here or nothing."

Lifting his head from her, he looked around them to see that night had fallen and they were well and truly hidden by the low-hanging canopy of the willow limbs.

"Is Matthew likely to come looking for us?" he asked.

She reached up to cradle his face with her hands. "Not a chance. He wants us to be alone." And to be in love, she silently added. The thought was so sharp and sweet it pierced her heart like an arrow. And she was forced to close her eyes to hide the sudden tears forming in her eyes.

Groaning deep in his throat, he looked down at her with one last moment of hesitation. "Are you sure?"

She hurriedly guided his hand to her breast, which was already throbbing, aching for the touch of his fingers. "Yes! Now, Seth! Hurry!"

The urgency in her voice was like a dose of gasoline on an already smoldering fire. All of a sudden he couldn't remove his or her jeans fast enough. His hands were clumsy and shaking and hers weren't much better as she tried to help him with boots and snaps and zippers.

Once their lower extremities were bared they forgot about their shirts and fell tangled together upon the soft grass where he continued to kiss her until they both had to tear their mouths away and gasp for air.

Once he'd regained his breath, Seth quickly rose to his knees and straddled her hips. "You're the most beautiful woman in the world. And you're mine," he growled with pleasure.

One hand delved beneath the hem of her tank top while the other found the heated vee between her thighs. Corrina arched toward the pleasure of his touch and wondered how she'd ever existed without him. He lit something inside her, something that didn't extinguish even after the coupling of their bodies was over.

"Seth, I—I'm not using any sort of birth control," she warned belatedly. "I—I never had any need for it."

His lips contorted into a semblance of a smile as the pain and the pleasure of wanting her mounted inside him like a giant tidal wave readying itself to crash on shore.

"I don't have any either," he admitted. "I didn't the other night. But it doesn't matter! It doesn't matter!"

She momentarily stiffened beneath him. "Seth! You—"

"Corrina, do you think I could stop now?" Even as he said the words, he was easing her thighs apart. "It's too late. I've got to have you. And—" he lowered his lips down to hers "—you've got to have me. Right?"

She didn't hesitate. She couldn't. Not when her body was wet and aching to have him inside her. She wrapped her arms around him and urged him closer. "Yes, Seth! Yes!"

He buried himself deeply within the soft, welcoming folds of her womanhood and the pleasure that washed over him was so intense, so incredible he threw his head back and groaned out loud. Then spurred by need, he began moving inside her, and as she wrapped her legs around him and met his hungry thrust, he was driven even more by the possibility of making her pregnant, of filling her body with his child.

In a matter of moments the rhythm of their bodies reached a fevered frenzy. Seth tried several times to slow the frantic pace, but it didn't work and all too soon he heard her cries of release and felt his own body being lifted, carried away by an explosion that rocked the very ground beneath him.

Sweat drenched his face and upper body. His starved lungs sucked in ragged breaths as he waited for the world to right itself. It wasn't until Corrina made a tiny moan that he realized most of his weight had collapsed on her.

Quickly, he rolled to the side of her. Brushing back her hair, he placed a row of kisses across her damp forehead. "Corrina, my sweetheart. My darling," he murmured.

"Seth."

His name came out in a raw, husky whisper and when he looked down at her face, he could see a single trail of tears slipping from the corner of her eyes. His heart swelled and emotion choked him.

"Corrina—I—" Slipping his fingers into her thick, curly hair, he stroked her scalp and pressed his cheek against hers. "I love you. You know that, don't you? I love you."

She went stone still, then slowly she pulled back from him and stared. "No! You can't!"

A wry smile touched his lips. "Why can't I?"

She breathed deeply and tried to calm her hammering heart. Seth loved her? No. It was too wonderful, too impossible to consider.

"Because…it's just not possible. That's all," she muttered. Then before he could stop her, she sat up and reached for her jeans.

"Why? You don't think I'm capable of loving a woman?"

His question didn't hold a bit of anger or frustration, but she almost wished it had. Dealing with the pain in her heart would be easier if he wasn't so gentle, so incredibly sweet.

"Of course I don't think that. You're a generous, loving man, Seth."

She got her jeans as far as her ankles, when she felt

his fingers against her arm. Glancing down at his hand, she saw he was offering her a white square of folded fabric. His handkerchief, she realized. To clean away the aftereffects of their lovemaking.

His thoughtfulness caused another wave of stinging tears to wash her eyes and she was glad he didn't press her for words as she finished dressing. At least the time gave her a chance to swallow away the choking tightness in her throat.

She was stuffing the soiled handkerchief in her jeans pocket when she felt him standing behind her, and she had to fight with herself to keep from turning and flinging her arms around him, confessing how much she loved him, too.

"Corrina," he said gently, "do you think I'm lying to you?"

Slowly, she turned to face him and her heart squeezed with hopeless pain as she looked up at his rugged face.

Licking her lips, she spoke in a strained voice, "I guess a part of me finds it hard to believe that you love me. But then I remember that you're an honest man and I—I have to believe you."

His eyes widened, then narrowed as he tried to make sense of her response. "Then what's wrong? I thought you'd be happy. I thought—" He halted abruptly as another thought struck him. "I guess I've been a little presumptuous, thinking that you felt the same way about me. But I guess you don't." He let out a heavy sigh. "I guess what happened between us a few moments ago was just sex for you."

"Stop it! Don't say that!" she cried hoarsely.

"Why?"

Anguish twisted her features and wrung a groan from

deep inside her. "Because it isn't true! What we shared was special! Beautiful!"

Relief flickered across his face and he reached out and curled his hands around her upper arms. "Then you do have feelings for me."

"I—" She broke off and swallowed as the true feelings in her heart rushed to come out. "You mean everything to me, Seth."

His fingers squeezed into her flesh. "I don't understand, Corrina. I tell you I love you and—"

"I don't want to hear it. Because it hurts too much, Seth."

Confusion puckered his forehead. "Hurts?"

She gave him a miserable nod. "Yes. To know that you care about me—but that we can't be together."

He bent his head slightly to peer straight into her eyes. "I don't think you understand, Corrina. When I tell you I love you it means I want you to be my wife. I want us to be a family and to give Matthew brothers and sisters."

Have babies? His babies? The idea thrilled her, filled her with a joy and excitement she'd not felt in years. Yet there was also pain and a weight of impossibility filling her heart.

"Seth, don't say these things." Bending her head, she covered her face with her hands and tried to ward off the helpless tears burning her eyes and throat.

"I have to say them, Corrina," he murmured. "I have to know why you have this idea that we can't be together." His thumb and forefinger came under her chin and lifted her face up to his. "Tell me," he gently commanded.

Amazed that he couldn't see the situation, she stared

at him. "Seth, you live in Texas. Your job, your life is there."

"I don't see any reason that you and Matthew couldn't move to Texas with me. I have a nice ranch with a house that's big enough to raise all the kids we'll want. I realize you have a job here that you might hate to give up, but you can finish getting your college degree and get that teaching job you've always wanted. As for Matthew's education, there's plenty of good schools in the area, both public and private. He can take his pick."

Corrina's mouth fell open. "You'd pay for Matthew to go to a private school?"

"Of course. If that's what he chose. I want him to be my son in every sense of the word. I want him and you to have everything you want and need."

She'd instinctively known he was a generous man, but to have that generosity directed at her was overwhelming, to say the least. Yet the financial security he was offering her was unimportant. His love was the true gift. Just to be able to live with him day after day, to sleep by his side, hear his voice and touch his hand, would be like getting the treasure at the end of the rainbow.

"You're not thinking, Seth. Do you think I can simply leave this place? What about my father?"

He made a palms-up gesture, as though her question was easy to answer. "He can come with us," he said. "It would give you the opportunity to get him some good medical attention."

The more he talked, the more stunned and incredulous she became. Her head swung back and forth. "You don't mean that, Seth. You wouldn't want my father in our lives. He—"

"Corrina," he interrupted, "I'm not blind. I understand your father has a drinking problem. He's not the first person to have one and he won't be the last. We'll get him some help. It'll be the best thing for him."

How could she resist a man who was offering her so much? How could she not give in when her heart was aching to accept a life with him?

"Oh, Seth," she whispered miserably, "Seth! Dad would never agree to leave here. This has been his home all of his life. And even if he would agree, it wouldn't work. It just wouldn't!"

Feeling as though she was being torn to shreds, she turned her back to him and drew in several long breaths to try to ease the awful ache in her chest.

For long minutes, Seth was silent, his face grim as he tried to absorb the finality of her words. "So in other words you're telling me that your father comes first, before me," he said in a thick voice.

Whirling back to him, she shook her head. "Don't do this to me, Seth! Don't try and make me choose! My father has no one to care for him but me. He's all the family I have!"

His nostrils flared with anger as his eyes combed her pinched features. "You're just like my sister, Victoria," he said flatly. "For years, she let our Dad use her. She turned her back on Jess and refused to move away with him because of our father. She couldn't see that Tucker was manipulating her heartstrings, playing on her sympathy with excuses of being in bad health and a lonely widower. It's all the same with you, Corrina. You're not Rube's keeper, so when are you going to wake up and start living your own life? Or is it easier to use him as an excuse?"

She let out a shocked gasp just as he turned away

from her. "What do you mean?" she cried hoarsely. "Do you think any of this is easy for me? Do you think taking care of him is always a pleasure?"

He glanced over his shoulder at her. "I'm sure it's not easy. But it's safe to you. This way, you won't have to deal with another Dale. You won't have to try to explain to another child why his father deserted him. That's your thinking, isn't it?"

Corrina swallowed as the truth of his words hit her hard. "That's an awful thing to say!"

"The truth generally is," he muttered, then reaching for her arm, he urged her toward the old cattle trail. "Come on, it's time we got back."

Thankfully, when they returned to the house, Matthew and Rube were engrossed in a television program and seemed not to notice that the two of them had been gone on their walk for a long time.

In the living room, Seth said his goodbyes to Matthew and promised to call him soon about another horseback ride.

"I'll be ready, Seth! And I'll bring my chaps and spurs this time!" Matthew eagerly promised.

"You come back to see us, boy," Rube invited from his easy chair. "It's nice to have a little company around here."

Seth nodded at the older man. "Thank you, Rube. Now I'd better be going."

Corrina followed him out the door and to his truck. Although she wasn't sure why she was making the effort. On their walk back to the house, he'd grown as distant as the San Juan Mountains and she sensed that he was anxious to get away from her. A fact that broke her heart even more.

As he opened the door to the truck, she stood to one

side and waited for him to say something, anything to acknowledge that she was there.

Finally, she said, "I'm sorry that you're angry with me, Seth."

Amazed by her statement, he turned, one hand resting on the edge of the door as he looked at her. "Corrina, what I'm feeling now is nothing close to anger."

There was pain and disgust in his voice, not to mention frustration and disappointment. She could have told him she was feeling all those things, too. But why bother? she glumly asked herself. He saw her as the problem. And she didn't have a clue how to fix it.

Moving closer, she touched his arm and the warmth and strength she felt flowing into her fingers made her want to step into his arms, to beg him to hold her and never let her go. She needed him. More than she'd ever needed anything or anyone. But she couldn't give in to that need. Not anymore.

"I don't want things to be like this, Seth," she said in a low, desperate voice. "I wish they were different! But I can't make them different!"

The muscles in his face didn't move. "Can't you?"

She groaned. "You make it all sound so simple, so easy. When really it's impossible. And I—I was foolish for not telling you that from the very beginning. But at first I didn't have any idea that you could be serious about me and then when I realized you were, I—well, I couldn't resist you."

He didn't say anything. Rather, he continued to look at her as though he were seeing her for the first time and he was thoroughly disappointed.

"I guess it was just my misfortune that I'm so irresistible, huh?"

The bitterness in his voice wounded her. "I guess I

deserved that.'' She looked away from him and swallowed. ''So…what happens now? Are you telling me it's over between us?''

Shaking his head, he groaned with dismay. He reached up to gently touch her cheek. ''You're the one who's told me it's over. But I'm not accepting that. I'm not giving up on you, on us having a life together.''

Her heart gave a hopeful little jerk, but she quickly tamped it down. No matter if he was determined, that still left the problem of her father.

''S-Seth,'' she whispered brokenly, ''I—I do love you. I love you terribly. I think—I think I've always loved you.''

Closing his eyes, he pulled her tightly against his chest and buried his face against her neck. ''And I love you, Corrina. I've been waiting to love you for a long, long time. And I can't let you go. Not now. Not ever.''

With his hands on her face, he tilted her head back and covered her lips with a long, hungry kiss. By the time he lifted his head, her cheeks were wet with tears.

''Seth, I—''

''Don't say anything else. Don't worry about it anymore tonight,'' he whispered gently and with the pads of his fingers he wiped at the salty moisture trickling from her eyes. ''I'll figure something out.''

She gave him a silent nod and he turned and climbed into his truck. But even after she'd watched him drive away, it was difficult to stop the flow of helpless tears and she was forced to linger in the yard, away from Matthew and Rube's prying eyes.

''Hey, Mom! Has Seth gone home?''

Drawing in a deep breath, she glanced over her shoulder to see her son calling to her from the porch.

''Yes. He's already gone.''

''Well, what are you doin' out here in the dark? Aren't you gonna come inside?''

A few minutes ago with Seth, she'd been dreaming, she mentally answered her son's question. That's what she'd been doing out here in the darkness. Dreaming of a life that was far from her reach.

But that was over and this was reality, she reminded herself as she walked back to her waiting son.

Chapter Twelve

For the next two days, Seth didn't have time to think about the Noah Rider case, much less work on it. A small emergency had cropped up on the T Bar K with shipping fever spreading through the horses and a goodly number of the cattle that had been penned at the ranch. As far as the local veterinarian could determine, the pneumonia-like disease had been brought in to the ranch by a horse buyer with an infected animal in his trailer.

Antibiotics and special care were being given to each ailing animal and it was taking every ranch hand available to separate the sick animals from the well, along with administering the drugs.

Seth had been doing all he could to help, and for the past two days he'd worked from sunup to sundown. The night before, Ross had called from the Caribbean and as soon as Seth had told him about the shipping fever, he'd insisted on coming home. But Seth had assured his brother that he and Linc were taking care of the problem and not to worry.

Thankfully this morning, Linc had walked up to the ranch house to share an early breakfast with Seth, and his cousin had given him the good news that all the animals appeared to be improving and there were no more new cases.

He only wished the problem with Corrina could be taken care of with something as simple as a dose of medicine. These past two days the woman had rarely left Seth's mind, which had made it even more difficult for him to concentrate on the sick livestock. He'd not seen or talked to her since the night he'd eaten supper at the Dawsons'. He'd wanted to drive into Aztec and make contact with her at the diner, but the shipping fever had made it impossible for him to leave the ranch. Several times he'd picked up the phone to call her, but each time he'd dropped the receiver back on its hook.

What was the use in calling, when he didn't know what to say? he asked himself grimly. To remind her that he loved her? She didn't seem to want to hear that from him. In fact, Seth had been searching his mind for the past two days trying to figure out what she *wanted* to hear from him.

He'd studied the situation from every angle and the only way he could ever see Corrina agreeing to marry him would be for him to quit his job as a Ranger and move back to San Juan County. It was not the direction he'd chosen for his life. He'd worked long, hard years to get where he was in the elite assembly of lawmen. It would kill him to give up his job, a job that had so far been his life. But it would also kill him to lose Corrina.

With a mental groan, he tried to shove the problem to the back of his mind and focus on the papers laid out in front of him. He was here to solve a murder case, he reminded himself, and he couldn't do it with his head in the clouds. He had to have more information, more clues than just those Jess had given him at the sheriff's office.

Rising from the jumbled desk, he walked across the study to stare out the long windows that looked down on the busy ranch yard. The sun was high in a morning sky dotted with high fluffy clouds. So far the day had been beautiful. Is this the way it had been when Noah Rider had ridden down into that arroyo with his killer? he wondered. Was the last thing he saw a bright New Mexican sky?

Spring in this state was very temperamental. Just when you thought it was going to stay warm, a northerner would blow in and cover the ground with snow. Although Seth had to assume that a man of Noah Rider's age wouldn't have agreed to go riding on a horse or in a four-wheel drive vehicle in threatening weather. But why was he on T Bar K land? Where was he going? Was he looking for something?

The questions rolling through Seth's mind were suddenly interrupted by the ringing phone on the desk.

Crossing the room, he lifted the receiver and barked a quick greeting into the mouthpiece.

"Seth? Is that you?"

The sound of his sister's voice caught him by surprise. For one brief moment he'd thought it was Corrina and his heart had soared with hope that she'd changed her mind, that she'd come to realize it was her right to live her life the way she chose. Not what Rube Dawson expected of her.

"It's me, Victoria. Why? Did I not sound like myself?"

She chuckled. "No, you sounded more like Ross when he's on one of his rampages."

He passed a hand over his forehead. "Sorry, sis. I was just doing some heavy thinking."

"And you must be exhausted," she said. "How are things going with the horses and cattle?"

"Much better. Linc came up to the house and had breakfast with me this morning. He says the animals are improving and the spread of the disease appears to have stopped."

She let out a sigh of relief. "Oh, I'm so glad to hear that. Now maybe Ross will relax and finish out his honeymoon."

"I hope so. It would be hell having him here underfoot," he joked.

Victoria laughed softly. "Well, I just thought I'd call and see how things are going. Are you feeling okay?"

A wry smile twisted his face. "Fine, Dr. Hastings. What about yourself? You know you're supposed to be taking it easy, watching out for my new little niece or nephew."

"Oh, I'm great. Just getting rounder every day. Jess thinks I'm beautiful like this, though," she said with amusement. "Can you imagine it?"

"Of course I can. You're the woman he loves and you're carrying his child." As soon as he said the words, images of Corrina waltzed in front of his vision. It was so easy to picture her waist thick with his child, the glow of impending motherhood on her face. After all these years, he'd never believed he'd have a yen for children. But if Corrina came to him this very day and told him she was pregnant with their child, he'd be thrilled to the core.

"Seth? Did you hear me?"

Victoria's questioning voice in his ear made him realize his thoughts had strayed from their conversation. "Uh, I didn't hear you. What were you saying, sis?"

She groaned good-naturedly. "I asked what you were doing when I called? I don't want to keep you."

"Oh." He glanced down at the desktop and the notes he'd written on Noah's case. "Don't worry about that. I was trying to put some clues together about Noah. But I've got to admit I'm not getting very far."

"Back in Texas, would you consider this a cold case?"

He thought about that for a moment. "Hmm. Well, it's darn close to being cold. There's not much to go on. When a detective is searching for a killer, he looks for opportunity, means and motive. The first two I can pretty much figure. Noah meets someone he knows and trusts. The murderer uses a small-caliber pistol, a .22 most likely. But it's the motive that I can't figure and that's the one thing that will open up this case. I keep thinking it has something to do with the money, but until I find out where and who it was going to, I'm in the dark."

"You mean the money that Noah withdrew from his bank account every month? The large sum?"

"Right," Seth replied.

"I don't know. But I'm wondering if there might be some useful information about Noah in some of the old ranch records. Maybe there's a name, a person that hasn't come to our mind that had dealings with Dad or Noah. We might look through some of the old bills of sale or whatever we might find," Victoria suggested.

With sudden attention, Seth straightened away from the desk. "I didn't realize there were records here that went back that far."

"I think so. Boxes of that kind of stuff are stacked away in the attic. No one's ever bothered to get rid of it."

"I'm going to have a look at it," he said quickly.

"I'll be winding up with my last patient in a few minutes. I'll come out and help you," she offered, excitement edging into her voice. "Wouldn't it be wonderful if we really did find a clue?"

"Miraculous is more like it," he said, "but I'm willing to try anything at this stage." He glanced at his watch. "It's not quite noon yet. I don't want you to miss any work to help me."

"You must have forgotten that I've started taking off the afternoons. Remember, I'm nearly five months pregnant."

He chuckled. "All right, sis. I'll see you in a little bit. And thanks for your help."

When she spoke again, he could hear a wide smile in her voice and at that moment he realized once again how very much he'd missed his family and how very much he wanted a family of his own—to be another extension of the Ketchum clan. But dear God, how was that ever going to happen as long as Rube had a grip on Corrina?

A little more than an hour later, Victoria arrived wearing jeans and an oversize chambray shirt over her growing belly.

"I hope you didn't wear that to work this morning," Seth teased as the two of them walked through the house.

She laughed. "Hardly. I changed before I left the office so that I'd be ready for climbing up in the attic."

Seth shot her a pointed look as the two of them headed down the hallway to the kitchen. "I'm not about to let you climb up into the attic. Not in your condition. Jess would kill me if something happened to you."

Victoria grabbed Seth's arm and gave it a loving shake. "No, he wouldn't. He's a lawman like you. He'd think it over before he put his hands around your throat and squeezed."

Seth chuckled. "Yeah. That makes me feel a whole lot better."

"Besides," she went on before he could argue, "a few years ago Dad had a good set of stairs built up to the attic. It's easy to get up there now. You'll see."

In the kitchen, in a corner of the ceiling near the back door, Seth opened a trap door and found a wide set of wooden stairs fixed on sturdy hinges. Once he had the stairs pulled down into the kitchen and steadied on the floor, he gestured to Victoria.

"All right, let's go up. But I want you directly on the step in front of me so that I can keep a tight hold on your waist. And for Pete's sake, keep your hands on the railings!"

As Victoria passed in front of him, she leaned over and pecked a kiss on his cheek. "Yes, brother. I'll be very careful."

Across the room, standing near the gas range, Marina stood with her hands on her hips, watching the two younger people prepare to climb the stairs.

"You two aren't gonna find anything up there," Marina warned.

"What makes you say that, Marina?" Victoria asked.

"Any kind of clue is better than what we have to work with right now."

Marina pressed her lips into a line of disapproval. "Well, you never know, you might not like what you find."

Frowning, Seth exchanged a puzzled look with his sister. "What's that supposed to mean, Marina? You sound like you did when you were carrying on about that howling coyote."

Marina walked over to the two of them and shook her finger. "I want to find out who killed Noah, too. But snoopin' around in your mama and daddy's papers is like eavesdropping. A person usually don't like what he hears."

Victoria waved a dismissive hand at her. "Marina, we're just going to look through the ranch's business papers that were collected down through the years. You act like we're going to be reading our parents' private diaries."

Marina snorted. "Amelia and Tucker didn't have time for that sort of nonsense. Besides, you won't find nothin' about Noah up in that mess."

Seth frowned at the stubborn cook. "Why do you say that, Marina? Do you already know something that we don't? If you do, tell us and save us from wasting time."

The question clearly insulted her. "No! But you two go on," she said with a dismissive flop of her hand. "No one listens to Marina anyway."

The older woman turned and walked out of the kitchen. Victoria shot her brother a rueful smile. "Don't pay her any mind, Seth. She's not really mad, you know. She just has her own ideas about things."

Seth sighed. "Yeah, and they're all negative." He

took a hold of his sister's arm and urged her toward the stairs. "Come on, let's get started."

The attic wasn't quite as messy as Seth had expected it to be but it was cluttered and dusty. He found an old folding lawn chair and set it up in an open spot next to a window. After they located the boxes of ranch documents, he carried them over to the chair and ordered Victoria to sit in it while he sat on the floor by her feet.

Together they began poring over the papers, searching for even the remotest clue to any past associations with Noah Rider. After two hours, all the names they'd found were ones they were already familiar with and Seth was getting discouraged.

"I guess I'm going to have to go down and apologize to Marina and tell her how right she was," Seth said as he skimmed through the ledger in his lap. "I'm not finding anything useful in this stuff."

Victoria leaned forward and stretched her back. "Well, we haven't gone through all of it yet."

"I know, but it's getting close to lunchtime. Let's take a break before we finish the rest," he suggested.

She nodded and then shot him an impish smile. "All right. But before we go down, I'd like to talk to you about something."

He looked at her with wary amusement. When his sister got that look, it could only mean she was about to ask him something very personal.

"All right," he said with an indulgent chuckle. "We haven't had a good old brother-sister talk in a long time. Just shoot ahead."

Grinning, she plucked at the shirt clinging to her rounded stomach. "Oh, I don't need to have a big talk. I was just wondering about Corrina Dawson. Marina tells me you've been courting her."

"Courting her?" His lips twisted to a wry line. "Well, I guess you could call it that."

A pleased look spread across Victoria's pretty features. "Oh, I'm so glad. She's a beautiful woman both inside and out. And she works so hard."

He placed the ledger aside and wiped his dusty hands on the legs of his jeans. "You're right. On both counts. Do you know her well?"

"Well, we're not what you'd call bosom buddies. But I visit with her from time to time when I'm in the Wagon Wheel. And she has visited the clinic." Victoria scowled thoughtfully. "That father of hers is something else, though. I can't do any more with him than Corrina can."

Seth nodded grimly. "When did you last see him? At the clinic, I mean?"

Victoria tapped a fingernail against the arm of the chair as she tried to remember. After a moment, she said, "It was in the spring. About two or three weeks before Noah Rider's body was discovered. Rube had cut his hand and wanted me to stitch it up for him. He told me he'd cut it on a piece of barbed wire, but I had my doubts about that story."

Seth studied his sister's face. "What makes you say that?"

She shrugged. "For one thing, I've seen plenty of barbed-wire cuts and this just didn't have the same look. The wound was too deep and filled with bits of gravel and dirt. Barbed wire leaves flecks of rust."

Seth winked at her. "Very observant, sis. We could use you in the Rangers."

She made a face at him, but he could see his compliment had pleased her.

"We doctors have to be observant, Seth. Some patients lie about everything. In order to help them, we have to be able to pick up on those kind of things.''

He nodded. "So how do you think Rube cut himself?''

Victoria rolled her eyes. "Well, I can only presume, but I think the man was drunk and fell on the ground. When he tried to catch his weight, his palm was split by a sharp rock.''

"Hmm. I wonder why he would make up a story about the wire?'' Seth mused more to himself than his sister.

Victoria snorted and the sound made it clear to Seth that she didn't hold much regard for Rube Dawson.

"Because he didn't want Corrina finding out he'd drunk so much he'd staggered around and hurt himself.''

Seth mulled that over for a moment. "You're probably right, sis.'' A regretful sigh slipped out of him and he slowly rose to his feet. "Emotionally, Rube is very dependent on Corrina. I can see that. And she's devoted to him. I can see that, too. I just can't understand it.''

Victoria studied his troubled face. "Seth, are you…getting serious about Corrina?''

Jamming his hands down into the pockets of his jeans, he moved a few steps over to the dusty window behind Victoria and stared down at the yard below. From this view, he could see the pretty little spot where he and Corrina had shared supper. That night she'd looked so beautiful in the waning twilight, the soft candlelight flickering across her face. If he'd not already been in love with her, he would have fallen like a rock.

"Yeah. I guess you could say I'm very serious about her. But…there are problems.''

Victoria twisted around in her seat so she could see

her brother's reaction. "Seth, when Marina told me about you and Corrina, I was so excited. You can't imagine how happy it made me to hear that you might have finally found someone to love. And now you're bursting my bubble with problems. What sort of problems? Her son, Matthew?"

Lifting his head, he directed a wan smile in Victoria's direction. "Hardly. Matthew and I are good buddies. He's a wonderful boy. And he wants his mother to be happy."

"In this day and age that's something to be admired. So if it's not Matthew, then what?"

Dragging his hands from his pockets, he walked back over to his sister's chair. "Victoria," he began in a careful, thoughtful voice, "when Jess asked you to marry him and go to Texas, you refused. You believed it was your duty to stay here and take care of Dad. You believed he needed you and that you were the only one who could take care of him, remember?"

Pained shadows crossed her face. "It's something I'll never forget. I nearly lost Jess because of that decision. I did lose him for four long years."

He squeezed her shoulder. "Well, I'm facing the same problem with Corrina. She refuses to even consider marrying me and moving to San Antonio. She says that she's all Rube has and she can't desert him."

"Rube could move with you," Victoria suggested, then added with a grimace, "That is, if you could put up with the man."

Seth wiped a weary hand across his face. "I've already suggested that to her. She says Rube would never go for it. And I'm pretty much inclined to agree with her. You can't take an old dog out of his territory and expect him to be happy."

"Seth, I'm so sorry." Rising to her feet, Victoria patted his arm. "Having gone through it, I can understand how Corrina feels. She's torn. But surely you two can work this out. There has to be some other alternative."

Seth shrugged. He'd never felt such a heavy weight of defeat on his shoulders. In the past, he'd always looked to the future with eager excitement; now it stretched before him like a gray, depressing sky.

"There is," he said dully. "I could leave the Rangers and stay here."

Stunned, Victoria stared at him. "No! You couldn't, Seth! That's your life. You couldn't give it up!"

His head swung helplessly back and forth. "I don't want to. But I don't want to lose Corrina either."

Empathy filled her eyes as she studied her brother's troubled face. "You must love her very much."

Meeting her gaze, he nodded soberly. "I do."

She continued to affectionately pat his arm. "When Marina told me about Corrina, I never suspected it was this serious between the two of you or that you were going through such torment. Why haven't you said something?"

He smiled ruefully. "I didn't come home to the ranch for any of this, Victoria. I came up here to help you and Ross deal with this murder case. I had no idea Corrina was even living close by. Seeing her was such a surprise. And I—" He let out a long breath and the rueful curve to his lips turned wry. "I guess I fell in love with her all over again."

Victoria's dark eyebrows arched with interest. "Again?"

"Yeah. I had a pretty serious crush on her back in

high school. But she wouldn't give me much more than small talk. Because I was a Ketchum," he added dourly.

Victoria chuckled. "I thought the girls went after you and Ross because you *were* Ketchums. And you're both good-looking, of course," she added in a joking, diplomatic way.

"Corrina believed Tucker would have forbidden the two of us to date. And who knows, maybe he would have tried it. He certainly stuck his foot in between you and Jess." Shaking his head, he slung his arm around her shoulder. "That's enough about that, anyway. I'm hungry and it smells like Marina is brewing fresh coffee. Let's go down and see."

"A person eating for two won't argue with that," she replied.

With his hand on her arm, he led her through a narrow opening of stacked boxes and junk.

"Somebody really ought to do something about cleaning out this attic," Seth muttered as he bent to push a bicycle wheel out of the way. "This should be in the garage. Not up here."

Victoria chuckled. "Be my guest. You might want to write that chore down for your next vacation."

He tossed the wheel toward an open spot to the left of them. Instead of his intended destination, the metal rim and wire spokes hit an old wooden table piled with several boxes. One of the cardboard containers toppled to the floor and a small, metal box tumbled out and spilled its entire contents of papers.

"Damn it! I've really made a mess now," Seth muttered. "Let's forget it and pick it up after we eat."

Victoria left his side and squatted over the scattered papers and envelopes. "Come on and help me, it will only take a minute, and we'll have the job over with."

Seth knelt down next to his sister and began to scoop up a portion of the envelopes. "What is this stuff anyway?"

"I thought it was some of Mother's old recipes but it's not. It looks like some sort of—" She paused as she turned one of the envelopes upright and read the address. "Personal correspondence from someone in Texas."

"Must be Aunt Celia. Mother wrote to her a lot." He opened one of the letters and began to read to himself at first. But after the typical greeting for her sister was over, Celia's words didn't make much sense, so he read them aloud to Victoria. "I'm happy to say your daughter is over her cold. It's good to see her giggling and gooing again. She knows she has a tooth now and delights in biting my finger—"

Completely puzzled, Seth glanced at his sister. "What is she talking about—your daughter. Did you ever stay with Aunt Celia when you were a baby?"

Victoria frowned. "I never heard Mother mention it. When was that letter written?"

Seth looked at the postmark on the envelope. "Twenty-five years ago."

"Then it couldn't have been me. I wasn't a baby then. I was in kindergarten."

They stared at each other in stunned silence. Finally Seth glanced back down at the letter as though he'd just stumbled onto a dangerous snake.

"Then what does she mean, your daughter?" he repeated in a half whisper. "How could Mother have had another child? We would have known about it!"

Victoria took a seat on the dusty floor and snatched up several of the scattered envelopes. "Read more,

Seth,'' she urged, ''and I'll see what I can find in some of these other letters.''

Lunch was forgotten as time ticked by and they dug deeper and deeper into the pile of spilled letters. Shocked by the secrets they were uncovering from the yellowed pages of correspondence, they couldn't stop reading.

''My God, Seth, here's one from Noah Rider to Mother!''

''Noah? What does it say?'' He reached for the letter, but Victoria held the pages tightly as she quickly scanned the carefully scrawled words.

''Oh—oh my goodness! Poor Mother. Poor Noah.'' Tears formed in her eyes as she looked up at her brother. ''It was him, Seth. Noah and Mother! Here, you won't have to read but a few lines to see how much he loved her. And from the sound of things, she must have loved him, too! But what about Daddy? Do you think he knew that his wife and his foreman were—were—'' She couldn't finish, instead, she broke off as she handed him the letter so that he could take a look for himself.

''Look, Victoria, this has been a shock to you and I don't want to add to it,'' he said gently. ''But neither do I want you to see Mother as the only bad parent here. Tucker had his share of women over the years. Ross and I knew it and I guess Mother must have known it, too, and decided to look for love outside her marriage.''

Dropping her head, Victoria rubbed a hand across her furrowed forehead. ''This is all so incredible. Our mother had an affair with Noah Rider! They had a child together! How could someone around here not have known?''

Forgetting the letter for a moment, Seth went to the

stairs and called down to the T Bar K's longtime cook. "Marina, come up here! We'd like to talk to you!"

A moment of silence passed before Marina ambled to the foot of the stairs and hollered up at him. "I not gonna climb no stairs, Seth. Not today. Today is bad day. Not lucky. You and Victoria come down here. Lunch is ready."

It was a bad day all right, Seth thought grimly. All these years he'd viewed his father in a poor light. He'd hated his philandering and resented him for not being completely devoted to his wife. But now he had to accept the fact that the mother he'd loved and respected was not the perfect woman he'd thought her to be. She'd not been faithful to Tucker and he had another sister out there somewhere to prove it!

Chapter Thirteen

Seth went over to Victoria and helped her to her feet. "Marina won't come up so we might as well go down," he told her. "We'll take a few of these letters with us. God knows we need something to explain this mess."

Down in the kitchen, the two siblings quickly imparted to Marina the shocking information they'd discovered in Amelia's private letters. The older woman went suddenly pale and grabbed her chest.

"See!" she cried. "What I tell you? Don't look in private things. You get hurt!"

She closed her eyes and rubbed her chest as though she was in excruciating pain. Concerned for the woman's health, Seth took her by the arm and firmly set her in a chair.

Victoria stepped forward and counted the pulse at Marina's wrist. "Are you having trouble breathing, Marina?"

Frowning with frustration, Marina waved at Victoria to step back away from her. "No! No! My heart, it hurts. Hurts for your mama. She couldn't even raise her own child. She had to let her sister do it for her. That must have killed her," she muttered. "Tucker needed his ass kicked."

Victoria was incredulous. "Marina, Mother was having an affair! It wasn't Daddy's baby. Do you think he should have accepted it into his home?"

"If he knew about the baby," she retorted, "he should have let her raise it here. Especially when everybody knows Tucker probably sired no tellin' how many babies of his own around these parts."

Victoria pulled out a nearby chair and sat down with a thump. "Well, I didn't have a clue that Daddy ever cheated on Mother. And I…wished I didn't know it!" The grimace on her face turned inquisitive as another thought struck her. She said to Seth, "I hadn't considered this before, but do you think this love affair had anything to do with Noah's death?"

Raking a hand through his hair, Seth walked over to the cabinet and poured two cups of coffee. "I doubt it. I just don't see any connection. That was years ago. Mother and Dad are both dead now. But—" He picked up the cups and carried them over to the table. As he handed one of the cups to Victoria, he went on, "I can't discount anything." He turned a pointed look on Marina. "Did you know about Mother? About the baby?"

Clearly insulted at being accused of keeping secrets, Marina shook her head. "No! Your mama would not tell me such a thing!"

"Maybe not," Seth said sharply. "But you might have suspected something was going on."

He pulled out a chair next to Victoria and sat down while Marina scowled at both of them.

"I did not pry in things like that. But I can tell you Amelia was a sad woman inside. She kept it hid, but I could tell. And when she left and stayed those few months in Texas, I thought she might not come back. I think Tucker thought it, too."

Seth and Victoria exchanged surprised glances.

"When was this, Marina?" Seth asked.

She drummed her large brown fingers against the tabletop. "I not sure. Victoria hadn't started school. Do you two remember that time she went away?"

Seth nodded slowly. "If I remember right, Aunt Celia developed some sort of cancer. She had to go through chemo treatments and Mom went to take care of her for a few months."

Victoria groaned with disbelief as the pieces of the puzzle began to fall into place. "Dear God, Aunt Celia probably hadn't even been ill. More than likely, Mother just used that excuse to get away from the ranch and have the baby without any of us ever guessing she was pregnant!"

"And Celia kept the baby girl and raised it as her own child," Seth added flatly.

"How you know that?" Marina asked.

Seth pointed to the letters he'd placed on the end of the table. "It's all in those, Marina."

Marina eyed the letters as though they were going to jump up and bite her. "So where is she now? This daughter of Amelia and Noah's?"

"Her name is Mary Katherine," Victoria answered. "And we don't know where she is. Celia passed away four or five years ago. But the letters stopped long before that. Mary Katherine was grown by that time. She could be anywhere.''

''And she not know she is related to you Ketchums?'' Marina asked, obviously as dumbfounded by this discovery as Seth and Victoria.

''We have no idea, Marina.'' Seth reached for the salad bowl. ''But if we're lucky, we might find another cache of letters up in the attic. Otherwise, we have a sister out there somewhere without a clue to find her except her name.''

He handed the bowl to Victoria, who picked up the wooden spoon and fork, then let them both drop back in the bowl.

She said, ''I'm not hungry, Seth. I don't think I can eat a bite.''

He shook his head at her. ''You were hungry earlier.''

''Yes, but that was before…before we found out about Mother,'' she said sadly. Bending her head, she pinched the bridge of her nose. ''I think I'll go call Jess and let him know what's happened.''

Seth gently rubbed a hand across her shoulder. ''Just think about the good side of things, Victoria, you have a sister.''

Just as she looked up and gave Seth a wobbly smile, someone knocked on the back door that opened onto the porch. Marina dragged herself out of the chair and went to answer it.

Anticipating that it was one of the ranch hands, Seth turned his attention to filling his plate with the cold meat and cheeses Marina had sliced to go with the salad greens. But after a moment he recognized Matthew's voice rattling at Marina a mile a minute.

"Who is that?" Victoria asked as Seth quickly rose from his chair.

Seth didn't have time to answer. Matthew burst into the kitchen and ran straight to him.

"Seth! Seth! I found Snip. I found him!"

The boy was heaving for air and sweat was rolling from the band of his hat and down his dusty face. His blue eyes were wide and dark with something that looked to Seth like downright fear.

Taking Matthew by the shoulders, he spoke quietly to the boy. "Calm down, Matthew. Take a moment to get your breath and then you can tell me."

By now Victoria was on her feet, and along with Seth, she watched with great concern as Matthew made an effort to draw in some much-needed oxygen.

Finally he wiped the back of his arm across his face, then latched both hands around Seth's forearm. "I'm okay now, Seth."

"How did you get here, Matthew? Did your mother bring you?"

The boy shook his head. "No, sir. I rode Blackjack over here—all the way! Mom was at work—at the diner—but she's probably home now. You've got to go there, Seth!" He tugged on Seth's arm. "Pa's in an uproar!"

Seth's eyes narrowed as fear flickered deep in his gut and pushed its way upward. "What do you mean in an uproar?"

Matthew squeezed his eyes in a long blink and it was then Seth realized the boy had been crying.

Glancing grimly at Victoria, he carefully put his arm around Matthew's slender shoulders. "It's okay, Matt," he said gently. "Just tell me what happened. From the very beginning."

Matthew sucked in another deep breath and nodded. "I was down by the stream. You know, the one where I caught the trout?"

The stream where he and Corrina had made love, Seth thought. How very long ago that seemed now, and how very empty he'd been ever since.

"Yes, I know," Seth said absently. "Go on."

"Well, I was ridin' Blackjack and I decided to go a bit farther than I usually go. So I rode west for a ways and then I found an arroyo with a little water in it and I rode down inside to give Blackjack a drink. That's when I saw Snip!"

Riveted by Matthew's disclosure, he focused on the boy's dirty face. "You're sure it was Ross's stallion?"

"Sure, I'm sure! He's a sorrel stallion with a white snip on his nose just like you described. And the T Bar K brand was on his left shoulder."

Seth didn't need more proof than that. "Was he running loose?"

Matthew swung his head back and forth. "That's what I couldn't understand, Seth. He was in a small pen. You know, the kind that you make with those portable fence things." Seth nodded that he understood and Matthew went on, "I knew it was him right off, so I hurried back home to call you. But once I got in the house Pa caught me and wanted to know where I'd been. I told him about Snip and he got all mad and said I shouldn't have been snoopin' around in things that wasn't a boy's business. I told him I was gonna call you and tell you where Snip was, but he wouldn't let me!"

Seth patted Matthew's shoulder as his mind raced ahead to what was going to have to be done. "How did you get away from your pa?"

"Well, he was all mad and cussin' about how he was gonna have to go move that stallion somewhere else. He stomped off to his bedroom and I thought he was goin' after a belt to whup me with, so I ran out of the house and jumped on my horse."

The kitchen went suddenly quiet, except for Marina, who was mumbling something about it being a bad day.

Seth guided Matthew over to Marina. "Show him the bathroom where he can wash up, Marina. And then feed him something." To Matthew he said, "Go with Marina. And don't worry anymore. I'll take care of things."

Matthew nodded and Marina led the shaken boy out of the kitchen. Once Matthew was out of earshot, Victoria whispered in a stricken voice, "What are you going to do, Seth? Did Rube steal Snip?"

His face like a piece of granite, he motioned for her to follow him through the house. Once inside his bedroom, he unlocked a small drawer and pulled out his pistol and leather holster. As he buckled it around his hips, he motioned to the telephone by the head of the bed.

"Call Jess. Tell him to meet me at Rube's as quickly as he can get there. And, Victoria, please take care of Matthew, will you?"

Fear gripped her face. "Of course. But what are you going to do?"

Hurrying out of the room, he answered, "The only thing I can do, sis. Arrest a horse thief."

The moment Corrina stepped into the house, she sensed that something was wrong. Matthew wasn't there to greet her and he never missed meeting her at the door. The television was off, something that never happened during the day. And there was no lunch mess left on the kitchen table. No one had eaten.

''Matthew?'' she called, then glanced out the window at the front yard. She had parked next to her father's pickup, hadn't she? Her mind had been so preoccupied, she could have just thought his old Dodge had been sitting there. But no, it was sitting right where it always did, so that meant her father was home. So where were he and Matthew?

After glancing in each room of the small house, she decided to go to her bedroom and change out of her uniform before she went outside to locate her son and father.

As she rifled through a drawer for a pair of old jeans, she tried to reassure herself there wasn't anything wrong. She just happened to be in a terrible frame of mind. The past two days her thoughts had been consumed with Seth and the problem that prevented them from living as husband and wife. She'd told Betty at work that she'd never felt more torn or miserable in her life and that had been an understatement. Being without Seth for two days had been torture. She must have been out of her mind to think she could continue as things had been before Seth had come home. There was no way she could live without him indefinitely. She was going to have to go to him, tell him all over again how very much she loved him and that somehow, someway they had to work through the problem together. If that meant approaching her father about moving to San Antonio, then she would do it.

The slam of a door suddenly interrupted Corrina's thoughts and she hurriedly pulled on a navy blue T-shirt and went out to see who had entered the house.

"Matthew? Dad? Where are you?" she called as she headed toward the kitchen.

There wasn't any answer, but she heard the clink of a glass. Rounding the kitchen door, she spotted her father standing at the counter. He was pouring Kentucky bourbon into a juice glass and drinking it down like water.

"Dad! What are you doing?"

He glanced around at her and she almost gasped. There was such a dazed, feral look on his face that she was actually afraid.

"Gettin' a little drink. Can't a man do that in his own house?"

She was used to Rube being belligerent with her, but there was something different about him today, something that made goose bumps ripple over her skin.

She walked into the middle of the room. "Where's Matthew?"

Rube made a sloppy wave toward the front of the house. "I don't know. I guess he went to see that Ranger of yours. Yeah, that's where the boy's gone. Gonna tell on his old pa. Tell him how his pa is a horse thief!"

Carrying the bottle and glass, he walked over to the table and pulled out a chair. As he flopped heavily onto the seat, Corrina walked to the nearest end of the table and stood facing her father.

"How much of that stuff have you had? And where did you get that whiskey? You never drink anything but beer."

He laughed. "I ain't drunk, daughter. Not by a long shot. And there's a lot of things about me that you don't know. A woman don't need to know everything a man does. It ain't natural."

She refrained from rolling her eyes and told herself to be patient. Something was wrong with him. He could have had some sort of ministroke and didn't know what he was saying or doing.

"Well, I think you need to explain what you meant about Matthew and Seth. Do you know for sure that Matt went to the T Bar K?"

He turned a narrowed eye on her. "Hell no, I don't know for sure! But the kid found that stallion and he couldn't wait to tell that Texas Ranger about it."

Frowning with puzzlement, she leaned toward her father. "Do you mean Snip? Matthew found Snip?"

Rube looked away from her, swallowed another drink of whiskey, then swiped the back of his hand across his mouth. "That's right," he said flatly. "Found him right here, down by the stream."

Corrina's stomach suddenly tightened into a hard knot. "Why would Snip be here? Dad, did you—did you take Snip?"

He refused to look at her and she could see his jaw working nervously and his hand tighten around the whiskey bottle. The knot in her stomach suddenly turned to nausea.

"Yeah, I took him. What of it? The Ketchums have more horses than they'll ever need. They got plenty of everything. One stallion isn't gonna make no difference to 'em."

She stared at him in stunned fascination. Her father might be guilty of liking alcohol and of being on the lazy side, but he wasn't a thief! She couldn't accept that!

"Dad! That horse belongs to Ross. It was his own personal horse. Not just one of the remuda! How could you have done such a thing? And why? I thought you liked the Ketchums!''

Shrugging one shoulder, he glanced at her. ''I do like the Ketchums, daughter. Me and Tucker were close for a lot of years. He was a cantankerous old bastard, but I liked him and he liked me. Didn't matter to him that I was always short on money. But then he died and everything changed after that—everything,'' he mumbled more to himself than to Corrina. ''Taking Snip wasn't nothin' personal. I just saw the horse one day and took him, that's all.''

Unexplained dread washed up in her like a black wave of floodwater. She couldn't bear to think her father had an evil streak inside him. But that was all she could think as her mind spun with questions. ''When? What were you doing on Ketchum land, Dad?''

He jumped up from the table and stalked toward the hallway. ''Don't you go askin' me things you don't need to know!''

''Dad!'' Corrina scrambled to her feet and hurried after him. ''I want you to go get Snip and take him home where he belongs. Maybe, just maybe the Ketchums will take pity on you and not press charges.''

He stopped his forward motion and turned to stare at her. ''Pity! I don't want any pity. Not from the Ketchums or anyone. And I ain't gonna take that stallion anywhere. He's mine now.''

In a gesture of frustrated defeat, Corrina smacked a hand against her forehead. ''Then you might as well get ready to do jail time.''

''Might as well,'' he muttered. ''Life ain't good like this.''

Dazed by her father's behavior, she watched him stagger toward his easy chair.

"Dad, you haven't answered me. Where did you get Snip? What were you doing on the T Bar K?"

For long minutes he stared off into space, then he seemed to shake himself out of the trance and filled the glass with the last of the bourbon. At least after this round he wouldn't be able to drink any more high-volume alcohol, Corrina thought desperately.

Rube swallowed the drink, then, planting his hands on his knees, he leaned toward Corrina. "I was ridin' Popcorn. She needed some exercise. And Noah said he didn't mind if we took horses over to the T Bar K ranch house. He rode every day anyway." He waved a hand at her and his voice lowered to a mumble. "Can you beat that? Noah was older than your old man, Corrina, but he worked at a feedlot, climbed in the saddle every day. Sure wish I could do that…sure wished I could."

Oh dear God, no! No, she silently screamed. Not her father! He couldn't kill anyone! Yet the story he was beginning to tell was sickeningly real.

Certain she was going to throw up, Corrina stumbled toward the couch and sank onto the cushion at one end. As she wiped a shaky hand through her hair, she said in a guarded voice, "I didn't know…that you'd seen Noah."

He cocked a clever grin at her. "Nobody else knew it either."

She had to be calm, she told herself. She had to go about this in a cool, psychological way. She couldn't just ask him outright if he'd murdered Noah, she had to coax him into whatever part of the story he was willing to tell and then hope the rest would come on its own.

"What, uh, was Noah doing up here?"

Rube snorted. "Hmmph. He thought he was gonna

pull a fast one on me. Thought he was gonna put a stop to payin' me. Told me flat out that he was finished. He was gonna go tell the Ketchums all about him and their mama havin' an affair.''

Corrina's mind whirled as it tried to assimilate the bits and pieces of information Rube was giving her. ''Noah and Amelia had an affair? When?''

Settling back in the easy chair, he propped his feet on a worn hassock. ''Oh, way back there. She was probably about forty or so at the time. But she was a looker. A real looker. I would have went after her myself. But your mama kept me on a tight leash and I—I guess I loved her too much to do that to her.'' The wry tone of his voice disappeared as he focused his thoughts back on Amelia and Noah. ''I heard 'em talkin' one day. Down at the horse barn in the tack room. They didn't know I was anywhere around and they were talkin' about her being pregnant and what they were goin' do about it. Noah was real crazy about Amelia. He'd do anything for her. He didn't want her to be hurt, especially because of him. He agreed to pay me so as I wouldn't tell anyone. And I didn't. Kept to my promise all these years,'' he said proudly. ''But then Amelia and Tucker died and Noah didn't see reason to keep the affair a secret anymore.''

Rube stared at her and she thought how he looked like a little boy explaining why he'd disobeyed his mother's warning not to leave the backyard. There was shame and regret on his face and a fatal hope that his daughter would understand his behavior.

''I had to do it, Corrina. I couldn't let him talk. Seth and Ross and Hugh—they would have killed me back then—they probably will now. But I wanted that money. I had to have it—for you and Matthew.''

This couldn't be happening, she thought wildly. But the shock of her father's revelations were setting in, making her shiver violently. Lifting her hand to her face, she felt hot tears trailing from the corners of her eyes.

She had to get to Seth! She had to tell him what her father had done. And she could only wonder how he was going to react. Would he ever believe that she was totally ignorant of her father's crime? Or would he think she'd deliberately hid her father's secret so he wouldn't be prosecuted?

He'd said he loved her, but he was a Texas Ranger first and foremost. He might not want to have any association with a killer's daughter. But she had to go to him. She had no other choice.

Rising from the couch, she went to her father and knelt beside the arm of his chair. Placing a hand on his forearm, she whispered strickenly, "Oh, Daddy, Matthew and I didn't need money."

The sigh that slipped past Rube's lips was a deflated sound and, with a sad smile, he stroked the top of her head. "I wanted to give you something, honey. I been savin' Noah's money all these years. It's in a safe-deposit box in the bank. I was going to tell you it was the money I got from sellin' the cattle—I just shouldn't have took that stallion. If I hadn't took him, nobody would have ever known. But I was on my way home and I ran smack into him. He was just so pretty I had to have him. I guess I've always been a sucker for good horseflesh."

Corrina studied her father's tired, wrinkled face and wondered why the past years had changed him so.

"Dad…I'm going to have to tell Seth about this. I can't keep it a secret from him."

Rube's eyes bulged as he turned them on his daughter. "No! You're not gonna tell him nothin' about this. If he figures it out on his own, then that's a different story. But I won't let my own daughter turn me in, no sir."

Deciding now wasn't the time to reason with him, Corrina started to rise to her feet, but he clamped a grip on her wrist.

"Where you goin', gal?"

In spite of his tight hold, she straightened to her full height. "I'm going to drive over to the T Bar K. I've got to find Matthew and make sure he's all right."

She'd barely gotten the last word out when he shoved her toward the couch. "You ain't goin' nowhere. You just sit there and we're gonna have us a long talk about what we're gonna do about this little problem."

While she'd been growing up, Rube had never laid an angry hand on her. She couldn't believe he would hurt her now. But then he'd swallowed nearly a pint of whiskey in a few short minutes. His thinking had to be altered from the ordinary.

"Little problem! Dad—" She stopped as she suddenly heard the sound of an approaching vehicle.

"Who the hell is that?" Rube barked out.

Jumping to her feet, she hurried to the living-room window and peered out. Her heart immediately swelled with love and fear as she watched Seth's truck brake to a halt next to her car.

"It's Seth," she said. "He's alone."

She watched him climb out of the truck and as she spotted the pistol strapped to his hips, she realized he'd come to take her father. Thank God Matthew had made it to the ranch to tell him about Snip. Still, he couldn't know the stolen horse was just the beginning of her father's deeds.

The creaking of her father's chair alerted her and she turned around to see him pulling a .30–.30 rifle down from a rack on the wall.

"Dad! What are you doing?" she practically screamed as he began to jam cartridges into the weapon.

"Get out of the way! Now!"

Corrina started to grab the rifle, but decided one of them might be killed if they tussled over the weapon. Nauseated with helpless fear, she backed to one side of the room while her father shoved up the window and called out to Seth.

"Don't come any closer, boy! I've got a Winchester aimed at you and I'll use it if I have to!"

Chapter Fourteen

Seth stopped in his tracks and searched the windows for a sign of Rube or the barrel of his rifle. "There's no need for this, Rube," he called out carefully. "You don't want to make more trouble for yourself."

"What do you care about that for?" Rube yelled. "You come to get me, didn't you?"

Seth calmly calculated the distance to the house and how much of a chance Rube had of getting a shot off before he could make it to the door.

"Yes, I've come to get you," he said to Rube, "but I don't want anyone to get hurt. Where's Corrina?"

"Right here in the room with me. She ain't gonna leave her old dad. Not at a time like this."

Cold fear washed up in his throat, but outwardly he was careful not to show so much as a flinch. He loved Corrina so much. Their life together was just starting. It had to be that way.

"Let her go, Rube. You don't want anything to happen to her."

"It won't. I'll see to that."

Seth prayed. *Dear God, I've got to think straight and I've got to think fast.*

"Rube, a horse isn't worth all this. I'm sure Ross will speak with the D.A. on your behalf. You'll get a light sentence, probably even probation. So don't make matters worse."

There was a long pause during which Seth thought he might see the door open and Rube step out on the porch. But it didn't happen and after a while the old man called out to him again.

"This ain't just about a horse, Seth. We both know that."

What in the world was Rube talking about now? Was it Corrina? Was he afraid Seth was going to take Corrina away from him?

"Then what is it about, Rube? You come on out here and tell me."

As Seth waited for the older man to answer, his mind began to churn with possible ways to get inside the house and end this standoff. One thing was certain, he had to get Corrina out of there and make sure she was out of harm's way. That was all that mattered to him. Arresting Rube could come later.

The sound of tires crunching on gravel had him looking over his shoulder to see Jess's truck followed by a squad car. Both vehicles skidded to a stop a few feet behind Seth's truck.

Taking a chance that Rube wouldn't shoot if he walked farther away from the house, Seth turned and trotted out to meet the other lawmen.

Jess's expression was full of concern as he climbed

from his truck. "What's going on here?" he asked Seth. "Victoria said this was about Snip."

By now Daniel Redwing had joined the two men and Seth gave the other lawman a polite nod.

"I'm glad you two are here. The old man's in the house with a rifle," Seth told them. "And he won't let Corrina come out."

"The bastard," Jess muttered. "What's the matter with him? Is he drunk?"

Seth released a long, shaky breath. "Probably. But that's not the real problem. He stole Snip and he knows I've found out about it."

"Oh hell, you're kidding!" Jess exclaimed.

"I wished I was." His face in a tight grimace, he lifted his hat from his head and swiped the back of his sleeve against his sweaty forehead. "I've got to get Corrina out of there, Jess. Do you think you and Daniel can keep him preoccupied while I work around to the back of the house?"

"Has he fired any shots?" Daniel Redwing asked.

Seth shook his head at the deputy. "Not yet. But he sounds drunk and I'm not sure what he might be capable of."

"All right," Jess said to Seth, then glanced at the deputy standing next to him. "I'll strike up a conversation with him. You get ready for anything. I—"

The undersheriff stopped whatever he was about to say and nudged Seth's shoulder. "Look!"

Whirling around, Seth saw Corrina running down the steps and stumbling over the rough ground to get to him. Weak with relief, he rushed out to meet her and she fell sobbing in his arms.

Not wanting to stay in the open line of fire, Seth quickly scooped her up and carried her to the back of the parked vehicles while the other two lawmen watched the house for signs that Rube was surrendering.

"It's all right, sweetheart," he said gently. "You're safe now. Everything is going to be all right." Easing her down on the ground, he wrapped his arms around her and she buried her face in the crook of his shoulder.

"He let me go! Told me to get out! Oh Seth—it's so—awful—"

Her shoulders shook and her breaths were shuddered as she clung to him and sobbed uncontrollably. Her pain was like a hot branding iron, searing right through his skin all the way to his soul. Desperate to console her, he stroked her curly hair and smoothed his fingers along her back as he murmured words of love and comfort.

Finally her sobs quieted and she tilted her head back and looked at him with sheer misery. "You don't understand, Seth. It's not just that—that Daddy stole Snip. I've got to tell you—I—"

She couldn't go on as more tears choked her throat and poured from her eyes.

"Tell me what, darling? Whatever it is can't be that bad."

She sucked back another sob and called on every ounce of strength she had to pull herself together. "Yes," she said numbly, "it is bad. Daddy killed Noah. He…told me all about it—just before you came. I was pressing him about the horse and he just seemed to snap. He started talking about Noah and your mother and how he knew about the two of them. He was using the secret to blackmail Noah. It must have gone on for years."

Until Amelia and Tucker died, Seth thought grimly as the clues began to fall into place and make sense. Once his parents were gone, Rube lost his leverage. It was surprising to him that the old man had managed to keep Noah handing out the money as long as he had.

Seth's jaw tightened as he thought about all the heartache and misery Rube had caused. Especially to his beautiful daughter, who'd always loved him unconditionally.

"I'm so sorry, darling. So sorry," he whispered next to her ear. "But it's over now and we'll make it through this—together."

Hope flickered in Corrina's heart and she opened her eyes and stared at him in wonder. "You mean, you believe me—that I didn't know about Dad before now?"

He groaned. "Corrina, how could you ever think I would doubt you? You aren't the sort of woman who would shelter a criminal. Even if he was your father."

"No. But I—I still love him, Seth. I know that's crazy after all that he's done. But he's old and sick. Mentally sick—"

Seth continued to gently rub her back. "I know," he murmured quietly. "I know, honey."

Across the way, Jess suddenly yelled, "Seth! I think you'd better come here!"

Both Corrina and Seth rose to their feet and looked in the direction of the house. Dark gray smoke was boiling out the open windows, while in one particular window, flames were beginning to lick out at the wooden siding.

Corrina gasped, then screamed, "Oh no! My father—he's—he's trying to kill himself, Seth!"

She lunged away from him and toward the house, but Seth quickly caught her around the waist and held her back.

"Corrina! You can't go in there!"

''But he'll die!'' She desperately strained against his hold, but after a moment, she realized she was too weak to struggle with him or the fire.

Once she limply surrendered, Seth handed her to Deputy Redwing. ''Whatever happens, don't let her go,'' Seth ordered.

''What are you going to do?'' Jess asked.

''I'm going in after him.''

Stepping in front of him, the undersheriff took Seth by the arm. ''Think about this, Seth. The place is full of smoke. Besides that, he might shoot you.''

''That's a chance I'll have to take,'' Seth said flatly, then pulling a bandanna out of his jeans pocket, he tied it around his nose and mouth and ran toward the house.

Corrina was so dazed it took her a moment to realize Seth's intentions. When it finally hit her that he was going into the burning house she screamed, ''No! Seth, come back!''

Absolute terror pumped adrenaline into her veins and with a sudden surge of strength, she tried to jerk away from Deputy Redwing. But the lawman was expecting her reaction and his hold on her arms was iron tight.

''You can't stop him, Ms. Dawson,'' he said. ''You'd only get yourself hurt.''

She watched in horror as Seth trotted around the side of the house and then disappeared behind the back of the structure. Jess followed him and positioned himself as close to the front door as he dared.

By now the flames of the fire had licked their way up the front of the house and were starting to crawl across the highly combustible shingles. In a matter of minutes the roof would be crashing in and no one would have a chance to get out alive.

She was going to lose her father. If not to the fire,

then to prison. Corrina had to accept that fact. But she could never, ever accept losing Seth. Without him, her life would be over.

Shivering violently, she leaned against Deputy Redwing and stared at the burning house.

"He'll be out soon," the deputy tried to assure her. "He knows what he's doing."

"He's not a fireman! He's—"

"A Texas Ranger," Redwing finished as though that made him superhuman.

But he wasn't superhuman and if he died it would be all her fault. Trying desperately to stem her sobs, she kept her eyes trained on the house. Long agonizing seconds ticked into two minutes, three minutes and then a loud crash drew her attention to one corner of the roof.

Rafters, plyboard and shingles were caving into the living room, sending flames and sparks high into the air. Too shocked to scream, she turned her face into the deputy's shoulder. She was praying so frantically she almost didn't hear Daniel Redwing when he spoke above the roar of the fire.

"Look, Ms. Dawson! Here they come!"

Twisting her head around she saw Seth helping her father away from the house. Rube was coughing violently, but except for a soot-smeared face, Seth appeared to be unaffected by the fire.

Sobbing with relief, she stumbled across the yard to meet them. Once she reached the two men, her father was too ashamed to even look at Corrina, but Seth put his arms around her and held her close.

Burying his face in the side of her hair, he said, "It's all right, darling. It's all over now."

At that moment, Jess stepped up and took Rube by the arm. As the undersheriff led him toward the patrol car, Corrina stared after the man that had ruined his life for her.

"My father—"

"Jess is taking him to jail, Corrina," Seth said soberly. "I'm afraid he'll be there for a long, long time."

"Yes. I'm afraid you're right," she said, her voice husky with tears. "But you saved his life, Seth. You saved my father's life."

Much later that night, Corrina lay in the crook of Seth's arm, her head pillowed on his shoulder. At the foot of the bed, beyond the wide window, the stars twinkled down on the high desert and a lonesome coyote howled to its mate.

Hearing the wild animal's call, Seth said, "I guess you were partly right when you said the coyote was warning us that something bad was going to happen." Drowsy from their lovemaking, he brushed his nose against her hair and breathed in the sweet scent of flowers. "But something good happened, too. That's what we have to dwell on now."

Stirring slightly in his arms, she rested her chin on his chest and looked up at him. "It was very nice of Maggie to let Matthew spend the night with Aaron. It will be good for him to be with his friend. And being with you like this is the best medicine I could ever have."

"Hmm. Maggie understood we needed time alone. And she knows all about dealing with little boys, too." He stroked the top of her head and then moved his hand onto her bare back. As it moved in gentle circles across her warm skin, he said, "I know your heart is aching over your father, Corrina. But I hope that soon you can see past all that and look forward to our future."

Her heart swelled with love for this man who had come to mean the whole world to her. "You know, Seth, it's hard to understand, but Dad always admired you—he always wanted you and I to be together. At least, he'll be getting that much," she said wistfully, then, placing her palm alongside his face, she added, "I'm so sorry I was so difficult before…about leaving Dad. I felt so—oh, I don't know, I guess you could call it beholden to him, simply because he was my father. But this morning, before all of this happened, I had decided to tell you that I couldn't live without you, that I would go with you to Texas, no matter what. Please believe me."

Bending his head, he pressed several kisses along her forehead. "And I had planned to tell you that I would give up being a Texas Ranger if it meant you marrying me. Please believe that."

She stared at him in complete wonder. "You would have done that for me?"

"I had no other choice," he murmured thickly. "Because I couldn't live without you."

She shimmied up his chest so that she could lay her cheek against his. "Today, when you went in the house after my father, I was terrified of losing you. I knew if you'd died in the fire, it would have been my fault and I could have never lived with that."

"Corrina, sweetheart, nothing would have been your fault. As long as I've got breath in me, I'm not going to stand by and let a man die. That's just not the code I live by."

Because he was a brave man, she thought. A good man. And one that she could count on to love and protect her for the rest of her life. Sighing with a content-ment she'd never felt before, she said, "I guess we both received shocks today. I learned my father was not even close to the man I'd always thought he was. And you learned your mother had loved a different man than your father.''

He made a sound that was something between a snort and a groan. ''And I have a half sister somewhere out there. Don't forget that.''

She rested her head in the crook of his shoulder. ''What are you going to do about that, Seth?''

''Find her. Just as soon as I can,'' he answered flatly, then before she realized his intentions, he flipped her onto her back and lowered his lips down to hers. ''Right now I have other things on my mind. Mostly, if you're going to be ready to marry me tomorrow.''

''Hmm,'' she purred as she ran her hands up and down his lean rib cage. ''Not if you don't let me get some sleep.''

His chuckle caressed her waiting lips. ''Sleep is something for babies. And right now we need to work on making one of our own.''

* * * * *

*Look for the missing sister's story
in Fall 2004, only from Stella Bagwell
and Silhouette Special Edition, as*
MEN OF THE WEST *continues!*

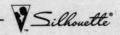

SPECIAL EDITION™

From award-winning author
MARIE FERRARELLA

Diamonds and Deceptions
(Silhouette Special Edition #1627)

When embittered private investigator
Mark Banning came to San Francisco in
search of a crucial witness, he didn't expect
to fall in love with beautiful bookworm
Brooke Moss—daughter of the very man he
was searching for. Mark did everything in his
power to keep Brooke out of his investigation,
but ultimately had to face the truth—he couldn't
do his job without breaking her heart....

THE PARKS EMPIRE

DARK SECRETS.
OLD LIES.
NEW LOVES.

Available at your favorite retail outlet.

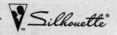

SPECIAL EDITION™

**Two's company...
but three's a family.**

Don't miss the latest from

TERESA SOUTHWICK!

After her husband's death, mom-to-be Thea Bell had given up on passion. Until she met Scott Matthews. But her craving for the hunky contractor was one she had to resist, for her baby's sake. Because she wouldn't let a carefree bachelor disrupt her dreams of a happy home—even if he was the family man she'd always wanted.

It Takes Three
(Silhouette Special Edition #1631)

*Available August 2004
at your favorite retail outlet.*

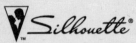
Silhouette®

COMING NEXT MONTH

SSECNM0704